Wedding Night

a novel by
GARY DEVON

LARGE PRINT BOOK CLUB EDITION

Simon & Schuster

NEW YORK LONDON TORONTO SYDNEY TOKYO SINGAPORE

This Large Print Edition, prepared especially for Doubleday Book & Music Clubs, Inc., contains the complete, unabridged text of the original Publisher's Edition.

SIMON & SCHUSTER
Rockefeller Center
1230 Avenue of the Americas
New York, NY 10020

Copyright © 1995 by Gary Devon
All rights reserved,
including the right of reproduction
in whole or in part in any form.

SIMON & SCHUSTER and colophon are registered trademarks of Simon & Schuster Inc.

Designed by Elina D. Nudelman

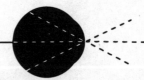

**This Large Print Book carries the
Seal of Approval of N.A.V.H.**

Manufactured in the United States of America

ISBN 0-684-80183-3

With love
to the memory of my father,
who, when he most wanted to go, stayed.

Like one that on a lonesome road
Doth walk in fear and dread,
And having once turned round walks on,
And no more turns his head;
Because he knows, a frightful fiend
Doth close behind him tread.

—Coleridge

Prologue: Eight Years Ago
Gardendale, Michigan

Once there was land—fields where they played and at night fireflies in a mason jar, and a woods nearby, blue with fog in the evening, the earth wetter between the trees, softer and patched with fern and moss. Winter was school and homework and in bed by 8:30, but in the summertime it was always after dark and the crickets were chirping before the children straggled toward home, ranging down the starlit sidewalks.

No one told them not to go into the alleyway between Marigold and Ninth, no one had to. The children knew. And yet, silently, like moths drawn to flickering flame, they gathered there night after night. "I dare you," they whispered, "I dare you," and when they were five or six strong, the children crept down the deep green throat of the alley.

Moving like the darkness itself, they darted toward the fence behind the rich man's house, the house with the bars on the upstairs windows. Iron bars. That's where they kept the boy now, the boy who had murdered that woman.

With firewood tumbling out from under their feet, they had to scramble to the top the woodpile if they were going to see him over the roof of the garage. And then they began softly to call to him, in small night voices at first, mewing and whimpering and wailing like cats until all their noises joined into one slow, steady chant, "Kil . . . ler, Kil . . . ler," and his shadow spread across that high ceiling as he came to the window . . .

. . . and began to scream.

The Present
Vancouver, British Columbia

"I've finally found him," the detective said.

"God . . . where?"

"In Los Angeles. He's changed his name to Malcolm Rhodes."

"You're sure it's him?"

"I'm positive. It's him, all right. He's getting married."

Silence. "Who's the girl?"

"She's an actress. On her way up."

The hand that held the phone was actually trembling. "Excuse me a moment." In a gentler voice, Preston Harwood said, "Evelyn, you've listened long enough; hang up the phone now." He waited until he heard the click on the extension upstairs. "I'm sorry," he said. "My wife has a bad habit of eavesdropping." Again, he paused to make certain she didn't come back on before he said, "All right, Stratton, I'll make arrangements to fly out this evening. I'll need your files, whatever you have. I'll take it from here, when I get to California."

"You've got to be careful, Mr. Harwood. He's killed before. It's in him."

"No one has to tell me about my son."

They were about to hang up when Stratton said, "One last thing. Somebody else's looking into this case—maybe you're already aware of this."

"No, I'm not."

"Some guy named Emery Hudson. He's been nosing around, asking questions."

"Okay, I'll have it looked into. Where's this wedding being held?"

"That's a big secret, very hush-hush. I think I've got a lead on it—if I'm right, it'll be at a private estate on Lake Arrowhead."

"Can it be stopped?"

"I don't know. Maybe. If you're lucky."

"All right. Keep me informed if there's any change. I'll be in touch with you as soon as I'm squared away."

When the line went dead, Harwood placed two quick calls to start making preparations—the first to his secretary to arrange for a charter flight and to instruct her about a room at the Beverly Wilshire, and the second to the garage to have his car brought around in an hour. He couldn't think about going up to his wife now. After waiting so long for this news, he stood for a long time, covering his eyes with his hands. *How could they let him out? It was madness! Madness, to let him go!* For three years now Harwood had waited for the call to come, and yet it was still a terrible shock now that it had actually happened.

It seemed strange that his thoughts were not more crowded and savage, but instead he felt hollow. This time he knew there could be no turning back, no pity, no remorse. He wondered if he could live through it again. All the old pain and recriminations came flooding back. He cursed under his breath.

Harwood was cold. He opened his eyes and the world beyond the windows was opaque with slow-swirling fog. In the distance, like sound buried under water, a bell tolled seven o'clock. When he leaned close to peer out the window, all he could see was his own face, fifty-seven years old, a strong masculine face swimming on the dim glass. Someone was out there. Only by

straining could he make out who it was—
the neighbor's boy, his head tucked into a
bright red coat-collar. Harwood remembered another solitary boy running through
the fog, dragging his book satchel on the
wet side street.

Behind him, the maid's approaching
footsteps interrupted his thoughts. "Would
you like to have your dinner served now,
Mr. Harwood—before I go?"

"I don't think I'll be having dinner this
evening, Marie. I've just had some upset-
ting news and I'm feeling a little queasy at
the moment. Thank you all the same."

"Very well, sir. Mrs. Harwood's tray is
ready."

"Would you quickly prepare my suitcase? The usual things, Marie. You know
what to do?"

"How long will you be away, sir?"

"I'm not sure. One of the larger suitcases will do. I'll manage."

The dinner tray was arranged for his
wife's convenience. The coffee was meted
out exactly for one cube of sugar and one
spoonful of cream; her fruit juice in its paper
cup sat covered with a little frilly paper cap.
The paper plate, the plastic utensils were

precisely laid. The cold orderliness of the slices of roast beef, the whipped potatoes, the perfect scarlet of the stewed tomatoes —it looked like a child's pretend dinner. He grasped the tray in his powerful hands and went down the hall to the elevator and rode up to the third story of the house. With a key from his vest pocket, he unlocked the bedroom door, stepped inside and locked it behind him.

The lamps on either side of the single bed looked small and separate, the glow confined to the pink silk shades. His wife was waiting for him. In her dotted swiss negligee, she held out her arms, the gauze bandages on her wrists almost hidden in her sleeves, and he came across the room. He put her tray aside on the hassock and kissed her forehead and then pulled a chair closer to the side of the bed and took her hand in his. She watched him with sea-cold eyes. After a moment, as if a switch had been thrown, she seemed to brighten. "They've found him . . . they've found my little boy?" she said in an anxious voice.

"Yes," he said. "I don't want you to worry."

"Well, I—" She tried to lift a lock of hair

back into place, but her hand shook so badly it fell. Not a good sign, he thought.

"He's getting married," she said.

Harwood looked at her. ". . . and that changes everything, doesn't it? Now there's someone else."

"I can't let them . . . I don't want them to see me like this, Preston," she said.

He could think of nothing else to say to her, so he kissed her hand. So much of the time she lived beyond his words.

"I'll get back as soon as I can."

"I didn't mean to listen. I couldn't help myself."

"I know, I know." Harwood cleared his throat again. He could sense her waiting. "I won't be gone very long. You'll see. Time will fly by."

"What are you going to do?"

"I have some business to take care of. That's all."

She sobbed a single deep breath. "Oh, how can I not worry? You're going after him. I know. You frighten me to death."

"You know what he's like," he said, "what he's capable of." He heard his own ragged breath. "The courts let him go . . . just let him go. They should've kept out of it and left us alone. He never would've got out of here. The boy's dangerous. He's dangerous."

She reached over and touched his shoulder, delicately, almost as if he and the boy were the same to her. "Don't say that. Don't you remember, Preston, how the three of us—we had good times, too."

"I try not to remember," he said.

A key rattled in the lock. Without knocking, Vivian opened the door. "Evening, Miss Evelyn; evening, Mr. Harwood," she said, locking the door behind her. She busied herself, fluffing Evelyn's pillows, stacking them behind her, telling her to sit up straight.

"How are you, Vivian?"

"Not too bad, Mr. Harwood." She brought the tray over and placed it squarely across Evelyn on the bed. "Old aches and pains, I guess. But we're all gonna be doing fine now, aren't we, Miss Evelyn?"

She was a tall, strong, black nurse in her late fifties, who saved her warmth and devotion for his wife, her precious little baby girl, Miss Evelyn. While she went about coaxing the woman to have her dinner, Vivian looked at him, as she did most every evening, saying silently what was long since written in her eyes: careful now, Mr. Harwood, don't you make our baby tired, don't you overstay yourself, don't you say anything that would upset her. This is awful thin ice we are skating on here. You know what she's liable to do.

After she had given Evelyn her medication and watched her wash it down with a paper cup of water, she retreated to her place by the door, leaving them to their nightly good-nights and sweet dreams.

Suddenly Harwood felt an uncontrollable urge to throw open the heavy drapes. He rose and his wife's desperate eyes followed him. The drapery whisked apart. Through the iron bars girding the windowpanes, the last of the sunlight was a glare in the fog.

"Was it the police that called?"

"No. A man I hired."

Tears threatened to spill from her eyes. Something terrible, ominous, hovered in her voice. "That woman . . . I remember. It was awful . . . so unbelievable . . ."

Harwood couldn't answer. He realized he was breathing shallowly, his body tense. *Madness, to let him go. Madness. Madness.*

"I wish you'd stay home," she was saying. "Oh, I wish . . ."

When Evelyn reached for her paper cup, he looked at his watch. His allotted time with her was over. "I love you more than anyone," he said. He kissed her on the lips, pressed her hand warmly. "You have to stop worrying. I promised you I would always take care of this."

Again this evening she had found her way to tears. "Oh, I remember how it was . . . I remember . . . this is just like his room." Slowly her head turned and she was looking at the bars. "I'm so frightened."

He stayed beside her as Vivian rushed to sedate her and got her settled into bed. He wanted to bolt, but he felt compelled to stay. He couldn't bring himself to look at his wife again until her incoherent mumbling had stopped and she had fallen into a deep drugged sleep. Even then, lying in that state, she was unbelievably beautiful, her rich black hair streaked with silver.

He spent a few minutes giving instructions to Vivian and returned quickly downstairs. Now the house was utterly quiet. Tall ceilings. Cavernous air-conditioned rooms. He took up his hat and raincoat, put out the lights, and stood for a minute in the orderly Federal living room, staring across the sofa at the windows.

The fog was less solid now; only a thin skein of it hung in the air and around the bases of trees. He felt the closing in of claustrophobia, as if the past had overtaken the present. He crossed the room. From behind books in the mahogany secretary he took down the semiautomatic and a box of cartridges. *Get this done, once and for all.* From a locked drawer, he removed a badly soiled manila file stuffed with papers and placed it in his briefcase.

Drawing on his raincoat, he went into the hall where a light was burning and where his one suitcase was waiting by the door. He knelt and slipped the gun and cartridges inside it. Suddenly it came to his mind as strong as a premonition—death waited for him on the other side of the door.

He was so absorbed in the sensation that he hardly noticed the doorbell ringing through the regions of the house like the sound of a soft drill. Harwood turned; he could see the distorted shape of a man outlined on the glass as he reached out and opened the door. The chauffeur touched his cap. "Good evening, sir," he said and reached down to take the suitcase.

"Yes, it is a good evening." The mist was changing to rain. "Airport, Roberts, if you don't mind."

Harwood got into the back of the Phantom Five and they were moving away smoothly, quickly, gaining speed: trees, hedges, his elegant house, all sank deeper and deeper into darkness, as he turned in his silent compartment for a long look back. The darkness sealed over him. At the inter- section, they sped through the traffic lights, where suddenly on the misty windows all around him, thousands of suspended red drops quivered and bled down the glass.

Day One—Afternoon
Lake Arrowhead

1

"**O**oooh, Callie," said Edie Garcia, one of her bridesmaids, "he's the best looking thing I've ever seen!"

"You've never *really* told us where you found him," Mary Dodd teasingly joined in the banter.

"Oh, I didn't find him," Callie answered. "He found me."

The kidding, the flattery and feigned jealousy had not stopped since the young women in Callie McKenna's wedding party started arriving early that Saturday morning. It was all lighthearted, meant to help her shake the jitters and she took everything they said with a grain of salt.

"She says she met him years ago . . . back at the University of Michigan." This was her friend since grade school, her maid of honor, Kristen Connell. She was sprawled across the bed, elbows bent, chin propped in cupped hands, blue eyes laughing with wickedness. "But don't believe a word of it. *I* never saw him in Ann Arbor."

Besides Kristen, Callie's three bridesmaids were Mary Keyes Dodd, her costar in *Blackspell,* Audrey Aquila, her agent, and up-and-coming costume designer, Edie Garcia. The women were in various stages of putting on Emanuel Ungaro gowns and matching wide-brim hats from Fran Hickman's boutique on Rodeo Drive—all in the prettiest, most delicate sea-foam green imaginable.

"So the truth comes out," Edie said.

"The truth is," Callie went on, "I had trouble remembering him myself. He's a lot different from back then. But, after all, I was different then, too. We all were."

Here in this elegant bedroom where she had lived as the guest of Emery and Dorothy Hudson for the last ten months, surrounded by her friends, Callie felt as if she were in her own private cocoon of normalcy. It brought back memories of the world she had left behind in Ann Arbor, joking with other girls, the stifled giggles, the whispering in bedrooms at all-night sorority parties. It had been a couple of years since she'd spent much time with women her own age, sharing confidences, laughter, and now, for these brief minutes, she was the center of the universe.

She had been awfully lucky, she was telling them, to get Mal. Malcolm Rhodes was absolutely what she wanted. Attended by two of the Hudsons' maids, a seamstress, a hair stylist, and a makeup man, Callie stood quietly while the dream unfolded around her. They were helping her on with the long, heavy, hand-beaded gown flown in from a London dressmaker.

She remembered the first kiss Malcolm had given her: he kissed the palm of her hand and folded her fingers over it. "Here's one to keep," he had said. She didn't tell the others how much he'd said he wanted her, needed her. How he'd said, "Let's get married as quickly as we can." Impossible to describe the evening, the moonlight. Or the lovely simplicity of the proposal from a man who must have known what loneliness was like—much as she did.

Two heaping armfuls of roses were delivered to the bedroom door. "Oh," she cried, "aren't they beautiful!" Even with the windows open, the roses immediately filled the second-story bedroom with their sweet, heavy scent. And from the veranda below, the first strains of Chopin drifted up, keeping the mood light.

As the florist left the room, the door was momentarily left ajar and Edie closed it. She turned in a rush to press it shut with her shoulder blades. "He's out there, in the hall. I just caught sight of him. Oh, Callie, can you believe you're actually doing this? Don't you love it?"

"Well, I didn't set out to get married," Callie smiled and said. "Three months ago nothing was farther from my mind. How was I to know I was about to fall in love?"

"You can still get out of it, you know," Kristen teased. On the middle finger of her left hand, she wore three glimmering wedding bands, the spoils of three failed marriages, none presently active, she was more than happy to declare. "I'll take over for you."

Callie laughed. "Oh, no, you won't, Kristen. It's my turn. He's mine. You've been married quite enough already." With Kristen, she often felt a leavening of humor was necessary. Kristen could be very opportunistic, and yet she always made Callie laugh with her irreverence—she still liked her for the easy familiarity of her cynicism and her merry malice.

All morning long Callie had been aware of how rapidly time was abandoning her. It was, she thought, completely disarming to be going through all the motions like this, when she'd always sworn that—when she got married—she wanted a small private ceremony in the Church. But with the press hounding her, a church wedding had become impossible. Ultimately she'd persuaded her priest, Father Cippola, to speak to the archbishop and when he understood her fears of her marriage becoming a media circus, she was granted a dispensation to hold the ceremony some place other than the Church.

Looking fragile and elegant, Dorothy Hudson, a petite brunette, separated herself from the nearest threesome who had just entered the room and came toward Callie, beaming, holding out her hand. "Oh, Callie," she said, "you spoil me. What beautiful roses; they smell of summer." She bent over the red blossoms and inhaled deeply.

"Careful, they have thorns," Callie

said. "But they're the ones Malcolm thought you'd like best. He picked them out and sends his love."

"Tell him he was right," Dorothy said, smiling. "I do love them." She was dressed in a gown of pearl-gray silk crepe; her hair was threaded with silver and beautifully coiffured. She surveyed the room with satisfaction. Everything was running smoothly, upstairs and down, she told Callie. No last-minute panic or confusion, no one trying to get in who didn't belong.

They found themselves for a moment removed from the others, just the two of them standing by the large, open window, and the older woman said to Callie, "Well, sweetheart, it's almost time to go. There's such a crowd . . . Tell me, quick. I know I shouldn't ask, but . . . Where will you be staying?"

"I'd tell you if only I *knew*. Honestly I would. I left that up to Malcolm. He wanted to plan things and I was happy to let him. So he hasn't told me anything. He wants it to be a big surprise. I'm sure we'll be driving somewhere, though . . . in that fabulous car you and Emery gave me."

"You couldn't've stayed right here, if

only we'd thought of it. We're going away, Emery and I. He has to go to New Orleans on business for a week or so and I decided to go with him. Imagine: no phones, no faxes—heaven! We'll be gone. And you two could've had the run of the place. Oh, I feel awful we didn't think of it sooner."

"Don't feel bad. You've given me so much as it is. Oh, Dorothy, I'm going to miss you." Callie hugged her all at once. Her emotions were excitable to begin with and the depth of the moment brought tears to her eyes. A year ago the Hudsons had been people she hardly knew, but when she was at such loose ends after her mother passed away and she had nowhere else to go, they had insisted she come stay with them.

"There, now," Dorothy was saying. "You'll be back soon." Then she laughed. "Don't pay any attention to me. I know you two would rather be off on your own. I understand. It's just all this trouble you have . . . with these idiot photographers."

Dorothy put her arm around Callie's shoulders, gently stroking her upper arm. "It's going to be sheer madness later on—you know that don't you? And, well, you're aware of how impatient Emery is. So why don't we say our good-byes now? I'm not sure what time we're leaving. We may not have another chance to talk for more than a minute."

Still, it was as if they delayed the farewell; they looked at each other and neither spoke.

Dorothy touched the bride's hand and leaned to her. "Good-bye," she whispered. "Godspeed."

"Good-bye," Callie said. "But, Dorothy, we'll be back in a couple of weeks, maybe sooner. I have to be on location by September twentieth, remember? If things aren't too hectic, maybe you'll grab a minute of calm with me later and help me out of this dress . . ."

"Maybe, so—" Dorothy Hudson smiled and the lines at the corners of her eyes crinkled. Callie quickly leaned forward and planted a warm, daughterly kiss on her cheek. "Thank you, Dorothy. Everything's perfect."

The woman squeezed her shoulder. "Let me know if you want anything. Now I've got to get back downstairs. I'll see you later."

Callie felt sudden tears fill her eyes. She was entering a new phase of her life, setting out on a thrilling uncharted path.

"Is it time?" Callie turned to ask Kristen. "Has he gone down yet?"

Edie, at the door, shook her head and waved Callie away and they all had to wait, confined in this bedroom, a little longer.

Kristen was saying, "Why don't you ask him to come in and say hello?"

"Oh, no, no, no," Callie protested, "that'd be bad luck . . . that's bad luck on a wedding day." She even started toward the door, to close it.

But Kristen was at the door and the door was open.

Suddenly there he was, walking by. Black tuxedo, white shirt, black tie, black hair, and joy in his eyes. With a fresh white smile, Malcolm Rhodes looked at her over the confused flotilla of sea-green hats.

Callie instinctively twisted away, glancing for a place to hide. But it was too late; their eyes had met. She had even seen him give a slight shrug of his shoulders and a wink, affectionate and amused, his playfulness unmistakable.

"Close the door! Close the door!" one

of the women shouted and the door swung shut.

Kristen gave a wild peal of embarrassed laughter and put her hand to her mouth. "Oh, I'm sorry, Callie. God knows I am. I didn't mean . . ."

As Callie tried to answer, the corners of her mouth were already beginning to twitch. "Oh, I know. I know. I shouldn't laugh." But she had started to, a little hysterically.

They were all giving in to it—all the women began laughing uproariously. The tension was broken. Leaning against bedposts and chairs and each other, they laughed and wiped wet cheeks with the backs of their hands.

Tears of laughter spilled from Callie's eyes, too. She wasn't really superstitious, although she had wanted to adhere to tradition. She knew she was laughing mostly from relief as she dabbed at her eyes with Kleenex. Finally she was able to say, "It's all right. It's all right. Years from now we'll still laugh about this."

It didn't matter now if the bride and groom saw each other. Almost recklessly, Callie looked out the big windows at the manicured lawn below and beyond to the gatehouse where the cars were checked as they came in. Her emotions were hardly stable. She saw one or two security men running around with walkie-talkies and clipboards. *The hordes of reporters and paparazzi were not coming after all.*

Every precaution had been taken: in Malibu, a shadow wedding had been created; rooms had been booked under pseudonyms; the florists were told that the wedding was for Emery's niece, and invitations were sent out late by special messenger. Now the limousines lined up, the valets were busily parking cars in the open field and guests were filing into the courtyard, which had been elaborately transformed with flowers.

Directly below, the festivity was unfolding. In the foreground, she could see the immaculate children—the ring-bearer and the flower girl—awkward in formal clothes and uneasy with their responsibilities. They were presided over by their mothers until the procession came slowly together. Near the altar and the grotto of flowers, tuning up in a chorus of dissonance, was a string quartet. The wedding cake, a six-tier extravaganza trimmed in violets and bluebirds and ribbons of icing, like a cake for Cinderella, sat on its table, shaded under the colonnade.

Isolated, not easy to find, half covered with Virginia creeper, the house had been built on a courtyard. The main house stoc ' at one end, its two wings flanking a gracious interior garden, which was sometimes transformed into an elaborate croquet court. Since the day she had first arrived, the whole place—the views, the old-fashioned, genteel atmosphere, the soft summer light—seemed to welcome her. Callie had once imagined the place to be forbidding, but it had turned out to be more of a home than she could have ever believed, more beautiful and friendly. It sat on a peninsula of forty acres of land, surrounded on three sides by Lake Arrowhead—the perfect place for the private, intimate ceremony they wanted.

She felt so relieved—she and Malcolm and the Hudsons had worried about nothing; their fears had been little more than a paranoid fantasy. The onslaught of photographers hadn't materialized. It was all due to Dorothy. "Let me see to this," she had said. "I'll take care of it. I know exactly what to do. Remember: say nothing—you know nothing."

I'm so happy, Callie thought. The only thing missing was the opportunity to tell everyone we were getting married. I had to keep my mouth shut.

And that added to the unreality of the day.

With the bridesmaids assisting with her train, Callie McKenna made her way downstairs and along the stone-flagged main corridor, into the large, elaborately furnished living room, walls hung with eighteenth-century paintings. In her right hand, she carried a white prayer book and a silver rosary laced through her fingers. Something old, something new.

Fresh-cut bouquets of lilies and roses, her favorites, adorned every table. Dorothy had told her that except for private screenings, they seldom used this room in summer; she liked to keep it for a change of scene in the winter. It was more a book-filled den anyway than a living room, Callie thought, better suited to winter and long afternoons reading by a fire. There were worn Persian rugs on the floor, red leather chairs with their telltale hollows, and on an open desk, scripts in irregular stacks that looked as if Emery had been called away in the midst of reading them. Dorothy's collection of Dresden and crystal gleamed among the books behind the glass doors. Callie lingered now, in front of the multiple glass doors of the bookcases that lined the three walls, glimpsing the hazy reflection of a girl in a long, flowing, white dress—it was like a dream materializing.

She remembered a much smaller reflection in a mirror, long ago, dressed in white organza and tied at the back with a glowing white sash. She could still hear her mother saying, "Gracious, child. You've been in front of that mirror all morning." Mama had been braiding her hair into pigtails. "Yes, ma'am, you're the beauty," she'd said, combing and twisting the strands of hair, "and smart, too. You'll have to be smart, very, very smart . . ." How old had she been that time? Six? Yes, six or a little more.

Something suddenly broke inside Callie—the reflection of her beautiful gown, all the excitement, caused her to choke up as she struggled with the vivid memory. If only her mother could have been here. *She* would've approved of Malcolm. The twig did not fall very far from the tree. The bride was made in the image of her mother. Her hair was the same dark, dark red-gold, thick and shining and glorious, and she had the same green eyes.

Over her shoulder she saw the man who would give her away entering the room. Emery Hudson was a man of sixty or so, a little under medium height, well dressed, well fed, comfortably sleek. Always the rebel, today he was wearing an ivory-colored dinner jacket and charcoal trousers with a chalk stripe. His hair, which he wore nearly to his shoulders, had passed through several stages of blond-grayness. Sometimes it looked almost white, bleached to lifelessness by the sun, sometimes merely streaked by gray. Remarkably like some battered old lion, Callie thought, restless, on the prowl and needing a comb.

They stared at each other for some time before either moved and then he finally stopped staring and came toward her, took one of her hands and said, "My God, you are a picture."

She was twenty-two years old, a skilled

actress and yet she couldn't utter a word. She was so overcome.

He held her at arm's length and looked at her in her white gown and veil, at the bridal bouquet and the little gold earrings Dorothy had given her for a wedding gift. "We're down to it now, aren't we?" he said and grinned. "I still say: you don't know anything about him. I wish you'd wait and let me find out more . . ."

"You're too hard on him, Emery. He's almost finished with his finance degree. He'll make a terrific broker. He's already made a lot of money on the market. We'll be fine."

Callie lifted her fingers to his lips when he started to speak and whispered, "Sh-h-h. You don't understand. I love him. If it ever stopped or anything happened to him, I don't think I'd want to go on living."

"Honey, don't lose your head. All I'm saying is . . . your trouble has always been that you trust people too much."

I don't see that as a weakness, she wanted to say but again she couldn't find her voice for a moment and even when she did, it shifted key unexpectedly in the hu-

miliating way she'd thought she'd out-
grown. Emery didn't seem to notice.

"Be happy for me," she whispered.
"Please. It means so much to me."

She caught a whiff of the sweet es-
sence of Courvoisier on his breath. "I love
you, baby," he said. "I hope you know what
you're doing."

"I love you, too."

Callie turned, smiled and held out her
arm for him to take.

A hush had come over the garden—
other than the soft strains of music there
was hardly any sound at all. It was as
though a spell had fallen upon the place.
One by one, in the breathless blue afternoon, the bridesmaids went forward; they
were like figures in a mirage who take step
after step, without advancing.

Then there was no more music. Pure
electric silence. Father Cippola waited before the bower of roses. Callie knew she
was next. It's like a movie, she thought. Any
minute someone would shout, "Okay, *cut!*"
and she would find herself back under the
lunch tent with something cool to drink in
front of her.

The wedding march began, the music

swelled and she started down the aisle. She felt nervous and had to fight down her breathlessness. She walked slowly, shoulders square and splendid, the motion of her legs barely breaking the front of the dress. The guests turned and got to their feet until they were all standing in honor of the bride, Callie McKenna, who was coming down the aisle on the arm of Emery Vale Hudson, her mentor and friend.

The bridesmaids arrived and took their places flanking the priest, mounting the steps like the green froth of an ocean wave. The bridegroom was standing slightly to one side of the grotto of flowers; over the bridesmaids' drooping hats, she could see his face through her veil.

Callie was so happy she could feel her cheeks burning and her eyes shining. When Malcolm Rhodes took her hand and she rose to meet him, she knew she had never, not as a young girl sitting at her mother's mirror, not even in films when she had worn couture silks and Cartier diamonds, never been so spectacularly beautiful.

They turned toward the priest and stood side by side. In his black suit and white Roman collar, with his wire-rimmed glasses and clipped moustache, Father Cippola looked scholarly and worldly, in the way priests often were now. Callie had told him how much she loved the book of Ruth, and he was making it part of the ceremony. In a voice of great resonance, he led them through the passages, using the old language—as she had asked him to do.

"Entreat me not to leave thee or to return from following after thee; for whither thou goest, I shall go . . . whither thou lodgest, I shall lodge . . ."

One hand with perfect fingernails passed the bridal bouquet to the maid of honor; then her delicate hand lay in Malcolm's without pressure. She belonged to him. She was so sure of him that she found herself thinking of the night to come, the cover of darkness, the way they would be together. Although they were barely touching now, she was so aware of Malcolm it was as if she could feel the hard muscles of his belly and thighs, the dark hair on his chest, the roughness of his jaw when he hadn't shaved . . . God, she loved him. Love waited in her fingers, in her lips—love, untapped, uncontrollable love.

"Thy people shall be my people . . . and thy God, my God . . ."

The tabloids and the columns were always linking her with one man or another—usually her costars. Her fans would undoubtedly be surprised to know that she did not fall in love or in bed often or easily. Malcolm was the first man in over two years that she'd slept with. Even when she'd confessed it to Father Cippola, he'd just nodded. The church, he implied, understood such things better than it once did.

She believed in what she was doing; she believed that what was beginning here today would never be interrupted, not as long as she lived. When Callie McKenna looked at Father Cippola with that direct green gaze and repeated the words after him in that clear voice, no one who heard her could question how fervently she meant it.

"And where thou diest . . ." the priest intoned.

She was aware that Malcolm barely whispered those words, although her voice was steady and strong, and she looked into his eyes, into the depths of them where—when he felt things most deeply—it was like looking into a black fire. She blinked, for a moment unable to bear the intensity of it, tears welling up.

"*. . . I will die,*" Father Cippola continued, "*. . . and there will I be buried.*"

She recovered herself enough to repeat it after him, but Malcolm was silent, or if he spoke at all it was in a voice too low and husky for her to hear. He was, she thought, too moved to trust himself to speak.

The rest of it, the questions, the answers, the prayers, even the exchanging of vows and rings seemed almost anticlimactic. Father Cippola was saying, "Malcolm, you may kiss your bride," and the guests were applauding as her husband took her into his arms. His lips were so hot they almost burned her. She understood. She understood everything about him.

2

The wedding reception was probably no different from the hundreds of other receptions celebrated across California that Saturday afternoon. By four o'clock, the temperature inside the courtyard had reached ninety-five in the shade; Callie could actually see steam rising from the surrounding banks of flowers. The mingled scent hung in the air with a powerful intoxication. Servants in black uniforms eddied among the guests. There were buckets of champagne and several long toasts, the cutting of the cake, a stream of photographs both posed and candid, a few kisses that were too long or too wet and much conviviality, laughter and joking—some of the honeymoon jokes a little too coarse for even movie people.

Still, she was happy, she told Malcolm; she was deliriously happy. She had never been so high in her life. She kept trying to bring herself down to earth again, but it was no use. From time to time, one of the bridesmaids brought her a small plate of hors d'oeuvres, but she was only half conscious of putting the delicacies into her mouth. She was even less aware of those times when she set plates aside untouched. It took self control, but she tried to greet all the guests, tried to smile—though just as easily she could have burst into joyous tears. The guests, as it turned out, were all her friends—people she had worked with or knew in some passing unformalized way— or friends of the Hudsons. She and Malcolm had come close to having their first real argument when he refused to invite his family to the wedding. His only guest would be his best man, a bare acquaintance drafted for the occasion, who served as a witness and little else.

"I can't believe you won't invite your mother and father," she had complained.

"I'm estranged from my father and my mother only listens to him. They have their own life. They moved to Canada years ago. I don't want them around me. I'm on my own. Take my word for it, Callie. It's for the best."

"Isn't there someone else . . . someone you'd like to have here with you?"

"No. There's no one."

Even if Malcolm had no reason to love
his father, the man was still *his father* and
Callie had been brought up to observe certain rules, to uphold certain civilities. Apparently he hadn't. "Oh, come on, sweetheart.
Surely you can't hate your father that
much."

"Let's just say that I don't have much
in common with him. He can't be around
me. Just leave it alone. It's been like this for
a long time. You can't possibly understand."

"But how can it matter so much . . .
for only one afternoon?"

"It matters, Callie. It matters to me.
Let's leave it at that." More than his words,
it was his unspoken anger that had convinced her not to press any further.

But today all that had been swept into
the background.

A nine-piece orchestra had replaced
the quartet. Callie and Malcolm danced the
first dance, their wedding dance, and between them swirled the same sensuality as
when they'd met again—after nearly four

years—only a few short months ago. Everyone was watching them. Callie closed her eyes and laid her head on his shoulder, and they continued to dance, without a word, in each other's arms. They were so ardent in their love, so wildly passionate in their need for each other, that they found it nearly impossible to rein in their feelings in front of others.

Little by little other couples joined them in a stately waltz. She felt light and graceful in his arms. The garden became a crowded blur. When the vocalist began the next selection, she hardly had time to catch her breath before Emery bowed slightly and swept her off, no matter that his steps did not correspond to hers. If he had something on his mind, he covered by making light of it or by talking business. "Don't let anyone tell you different," he advised her. "You're just on the cusp, kiddo. One more hit and everyone will know your name. You'll have the world at your feet." He was getting increasingly mellow on his Courvoisier. "I don't want anyone to ever make you unhappy," he said.

"That's sweet," she said, earnestly, "but don't worry so much, Emery."

When the dance was over, Emery called to one of the maids, "Eva, would you bring me a vodka martini on ice? Very dry, please."

"What?" Callie teased him. "Not your beloved brandy?" and he laughed. When she was able to return to Malcolm, one of the older ladies was telling him, "The years may seem like a lot of time to you, but it doesn't look long from where I stand, looking back. Life slips so quickly through your fingers."

Malcolm smiled and said nothing. His eyes, Callie saw, were moving about the garden again, carefully, watchfully. A maid in a black dress and white apron served them glasses of champagne.

"Make the most of it while you can. Grasp it and savor it, my dear." The woman was practically shaking her fist at him. "Now—well, I see your bride is here. Good-bye . . ."

The afternoon wore gracefully on toward evening.

Often the bride and groom found themselves unavoidably separated, occasionally for several minutes at a time. At twenty-four, he could be feverish with excitement or, if necessary, cool and detached. But he was never far away from her. They looped arms and drank champagne, and he danced with her once with a rose between his teeth. Malcolm reveled in sweeping her away from tedious conversations, in tapping shoulders and cutting in on her handsome friends, in whisking her quickly behind the high banks of flowers and kissing her until her heart beat out of control. "I'm crazy about you," he kept telling her. "I can't stop. Let's get out of here!"

"We can't," she repeated. "Not yet."

All afternoon he was never able to satisfy his hunger for her. He nibbled her ear and said she was his entire world, that he lived for her. Even when they were separated, she could still feel his embrace, hear his whisper and almost burn with the fire of his kiss—wildness flashed between them as pure as electricity. She fanned herself and decided: I've got to stop thinking like this.

It was after five when she danced once more with Emery. Some minutes later, she was aware that he was following one of the maids from the courtyard on some mission.

Again and again Callie was swept out onto the dance floor, only to watch helplessly as Malcolm was drawn into another tedious round of talk. Or, trapped in the praise of admiring older ladies, she would look past their orchid corsages and catch sight of Malcolm talking and shaking hands with men who were a lifetime his senior. She would be a good wife to him; she was determined to follow where he led, to make his interests hers.

The sun was going down, the shadows lengthening in the courtyard. Out of the corner of her eye, Callie saw the luster of a gray gown cross behind a wall of guests. That was Dorothy, she thought. I'll have to thank her again for all this. She certainly pulled it off without a hitch.

But before she could politely excuse herself and make her way through the crowd, Kristen intercepted her and said, "I'm with Russell Palmer over there. You know Russell, don't you? I can't convince him we're old friends; he won't believe a word I say. Why don't you come over and say hello?"

Callie said maybe she would.

And by then, it was too late to get to

Dorothy Hudson, who was also leaving the courtyard, a few steps behind a maid. Callie watched her go in the same direction Emery had gone.

I wonder what's happening.

Then, inadvertently, Callie lost track of them. Someone was asking her a question and before she could complete the sentence or even try to answer it, she felt herself pressed to the stiff pleated front of a white shirt and borne away.

It might have been another half hour, perhaps no more than fifteen minutes, when she returned from dancing with Eddie Ketchum, the director. A thin rogue of a man, he had signed on to direct Emery's next film called *Transgression* and was making it a condition of his acceptance that she be offered the lead female role. She led him to believe that she could hardly contain her excitement, when actually her feelings about the project were far from resolved.

When the dance was over, she returned to the veranda only to find that Malcolm was gone. She rotated slowly on her toes, eyes searching the crowd.

Yes, there he was.

Callie was a little high from the champagne, but not too high to see that something was the matter. Near a bank of white chrysanthemums, Malcolm stood as straight and motionless as a dagger rammed into the ground, heels together, arms crossed tight. His face was frozen; Callie turned her eyes, following the direction of his gaze.

Through the windows across the way, she saw Dorothy and Emery standing in the seldom-used living room talking with someone. Apparently Malcolm could see who it was, but Callie's view was obstructed by partially drawn drapes. All she could make out were white cuffs, the dark sleeves of a dinner jacket and what appeared to be a man's hands. As far as she could tell, the three of them were talking. Nothing else. And yet, when she glanced back at Malcolm, his anxiety was so pronounced that unconsciously Callie found herself reproducing it on her own face. He stood staring at the three people in the living room with eyes so hard and full of hate that he seemed to drain away from her.

She started toward him and again she looked into the living room. The Hudsons were still there, still talking—heatedly, it appeared. As she watched, Emery ran his hand in a distraught way over the thinning hair on top of his head. Then they turned and withdrew from sight; apparently, Emery was showing the man out.

"What was that about?" she asked, gently, as she reached Malcolm.

He had a way of not answering questions he'd rather not deal with, brushing them aside or acting as if he hadn't heard.

"Tell me," she said, coaxingly. Callie put her hand on his shoulder and felt his back tighten with her touch. He didn't draw away, nor did he turn.

"Sweetheart, do you know who that was?"

After a few seconds, Malcolm shook his head.

"Then, what's the matter?" Callie let out a deep breath. "Please, darling . . . Mal, please come on. Whoever it is, let's pretend he's not there. Emery will handle it; believe me, he knows how."

When Malcolm turned and looked at her, Callie was struck by the transformation, by his sudden air of composure. "Well," he said, "these goddamned tabloid reporters . . .'' She saw that his hands were slightly trembling as he lit a cigarette.

"It's nothing," Callie told him. "Let's not talk about it anymore. Let's not even think about it." She found she was reluctant to look into his eyes for fear the spell would be broken. But one glance, one glance and he seemed to have lost all interest in everything but her. His eyes gazed down at her with love. Leaning over he kissed her tenderly on the lips. "All right, gorgeous," he said. "Let's not talk about it."

Callie stretched out her hands and, with an attempt at humor, said, "I know what you're thinking. You're thinking: now I've got to dance with her again."

When suddenly the orchestra started playing again she gave a quick little yelp of delight, turned to him and put hands on his shoulders. "Come on, darling," she said, "dance with me."

If there had been a thousand people in the courtyard as he led her out, Callie couldn't have felt more exposed. A moment later they were dancing. As he twirled her around, she could tell that Malcolm was stealing glances into the room. Callie grew more and more apprehensive. She was consumed with the haunting sensation that eyes, cold unfeeling eyes were watching them from somewhere.

"There's no need to think of them," she insisted. "Look at me. Look at me. Keep looking at me." She rested her cheek against his and spoke to him in a whisper. "Don't you know how happy I am?" she pleaded. "Don't break this spell. We'll never have this time again."

She felt a drop of rain strike her forehead and looked up. The thunder sounded distant but lightning flashed in the dark clouds gathering overhead. Another wet drop touched her face. Callie laughed shakily. It was only rain, tiny warning drops.

Once more, quickly, she spoke in a whisper. "If I told you I loved you here in the middle of this dance, would you think me ridiculous?"

"Never," Malcolm said. "Never, never."

Raindrops were beginning to pelt the Virginia creeper. An audible gasp went up from the crowd, then feminine shrieks broke out as guests in their finery scurried into the house or under cover of the large striped tent.

Suddenly it was raining hard—thin, gray sheets of rain slapping against the stone walls and windows and they were inside the long central hall of the mansion, brightly lit and crowded already with guests. Callie rose on tiptoe. "I love you so much," she said, "you'll see. I'll make everything all right."

The light in the garden had faded to dusk and the windows were dark with rain. Some of the guests were already leaving at the front door, their cars coming round for them. Callie and Malcolm said a few halting good-byes, but she knew they had reached the time when the bride and groom were supposed to make their getaway. It was supposed to be made difficult for them, but there wouldn't be much trouble here this evening. No one would try to abduct the bride or sabotage their car. Everything had been thoroughly planned in advance. As Callie caught her breath, she leaned to her groom and said, "Mal, everyone will start going home after this rain. Shouldn't we go up and change? It's almost seven-thirty."

"Why don't you go ahead and get started?" he replied. "I'll be along in a few minutes. I should say good-bye to Father Cippola."

"Oh . . . yes, it completely skipped my mind. Would you mind saying good-bye for me, too?"

"Of course not." He smiled. "I won't be long, but there's no use in your waiting."

And yet, she hesitated. Instinct kept whispering that something was wrong and she hated to leave him.

"All right," Callie answered at last, feeling suddenly desolate. She watched him leave her side and work his way through the crowd until a black sleeve with a white cuff —one of the maids, she realized—handed him a slip of blue paper. Malcolm unfolded it, glanced at it, turned abruptly and went back toward the French doors that led to the kitchen and outside.

It was her last glimpse, indistinct and hasty, of Malcolm's figure across the crowded foyer—on his way out, following the maid.

3

Gathering her long skirts, Callie ran up the stairs, stopping long enough to tell the maid to see if she could find Mrs. Hudson and ask her to come to the bride's bedroom. "And, would you please bring me the tallest glass of ice water in the house?"

"Yes, Miss McKenna," the maid said and turned to go.

Callie laughed. "Oh, I'm Mrs. Rhodes now."

"Of course. I'm sorry, Mrs. Rhodes."

"Consuela, one more thing—since you're here, would you mind helping me undo this dress? I can't stand it another minute."

"Yes, okay."

A heavy-set, white-capped woman carrying an armful of laundry slipped away while Callie entered the bedroom. Gifts from her wedding shower, only a few days ago, were stacked and scattered on the floor. A silver tray and two silver teapots winked in the lamplight. Vases of flowers were everywhere in the room. Callie felt wonderfully pampered and indulged.

Conseula was saying, "Where should we start? Maybe if you turned." The maid unsnapped the back of the heavy white dress, her fingers unhooking and unbuttoning.

"Thank you, Conseula. That's all I need for now."

As soon as the maid had gone, Callie slid the dress off her shoulders and let it fall; she crossed her arms and pulled the long slip up over her head. It was astonishing how much straighter she felt herself standing now.

In her bathrobe, she sat at the dressing table and began to take off her makeup that felt caked on her face. Outside, the direction of the wind had changed; she gazed at the window where gusts of rain were lashing against it.

The hard rain obscured the evening vista and drummed on the roof. On the other side of the room, the windows faced across the lake, where their car was awaiting them—hidden in a neighbor's garage—the view completely invisible now because of the rain.

Gradually she was conscious of altered sound, the hiss of rain among the foliage. Windows were open somewhere—rain blowing in. The paneled upstairs hall ran dimly toward the back of the house, where a door stood open to the master bedroom and a thin band of light shone through it. Callie listened for footsteps, for the opening and closing of doors, for voices, but there was no sound. Strange. A house full of people—and silence.

In the Hudsons' bedroom, only one of the small bedside lamps had been left on. The light was inadequate for the big room, leaving the ceiling and the corners in shadow. The north-facing windows had been left open and rain was pouring in on the waxed hardwood floor. In the flashes of lightning, it shone like a wet brown skin. "Dorothy?" she said quietly. "Dorothy, are you in here?" The bedroom walls were ghostly gray and the furniture rippled as if under a rapid current. "Dorothy?"

Callie quickly crossed the room and shut the two windows. The frames were so wet that her hands slipped as she grasped one of them and the window came down with a hard, loud thud on the flooded sill.

As she was about to turn away, she noticed Dorothy's handbag lying on the carpet off the side of the bed. Its clasp had sprung open; as she picked it up, the black satin jaws spilled lipstick, Dentyne gum, a lace handkerchief, a mirror, an address book in red morocco. At the same time, the purse gave out an aroma—an aroma concocted from its many contents—that floated about her for a moment, arousing in her a startling memory of intimacy. Her mother's handbag had smelled exactly like this. Callie wanted to bury her face in that purse and drink in the scent—the scent of pure sweet remembrance. Her eyes filled with burning tears; unexpectedly, after struggling all afternoon to keep her grief at bay, she piercingly wanted her mother to be there.

Suddenly it struck her as never before —she was alone. Absolutely alone. Except for Malcolm. Up till now, she had thought herself to be self-sufficient, but her mother had always been there behind her, her love had always been there—Callie had had someone, a mother, a home.

Rain was still coming down heavily but the storm was veering away now and the flashes of lightning were like echoes of light in the dark clouds. Callie was on her way back to her room when she looked up and saw Malcolm appear at the far end of the corridor as if he had come up through a trap door.

"You look wonderful, Mrs. Rhodes," he said as he came toward her. "God, I forgot how beautiful you are."

"Wait till I'm dressed. Then I'll be beautiful."

He laughed. "Wait a minute. That's not how it works." He seemed to be bursting with happiness as his eyes took in the contents of the upstairs hallway, piece by piece. He leaned forward and kissed her on the tip of her nose. "I've got to get out of these clothes. Look at me. I'm soaked." His face, his voice were almost tingling with excitement, she thought.

"Is everything all right?"

"Yes. Never better. Why wouldn't it be?"

She followed him into the master bedroom, where he had changed clothes earlier and where his clothes were laid out for him now. She got one of the big white bathrobes from the linen closet and took it to him.

"I don't want you catching a cold—not tonight."

She watched as he unbuttoned his wet shirt, removed the studs, then the cuff links, his face a mask of concentration. Now that he was here, Callie felt some of her tension leaving her, like a piece of ice melting inside her. "I was wondering," she said, "did you by any chance see Dorothy when you came up?"

He shrugged and shook his head. "No, I didn't see either of them." He put on the bathrobe and knotted the sash. Turning his back to her, Malcolm stepped out of his trousers and emptied his pockets, transferring their contents to the clean, dry trousers he would wear.

"But . . . look," Callie said. "She left her purse behind."

"I wouldn't lug that thing around all day, would you? She probably changed purses."

"I guess you're right. That's what I was thinking."

As Malcolm bent over to remove his shoes, his head was a mass of pure wet black and she wanted to thrust her face down into it and let herself speak with tenderness of many things. Instead she smiled and said, "I can offer you a cognac. We have Emery's Courvoisier. Or is there something else you'd rather have?" She moved close as he turned toward her. "This, for instance?" she said and kissed him lightly for only a second or two and broke away.

But before she could leave the room he had circled her body from behind, hands upon her breasts, and pressed his lips to the nape of her neck. His fingers slipped inside the soft lapels and pushed the robe down over her shoulders. She said, "Uh-uh," and lifted his hands away, but otherwise didn't move. Holding his hand at a little distance she stood submitting to his lips and the close proximity of his body. She knew she couldn't let it last for long.

"We can't do this . . . here," she groaned softly. "Someone will come in, sure as hell." She freed herself from him and laughed. "Besides, I'll never get dressed if you keep it up. Just kiss me once more and then go get your shower."

"I think we'd better hurry and get out of here," he said into Callie's ear. "You taste too good."

"I'll be a few minutes yet," she told him, then slipped away. "You know it always takes me a long time. And you're not ready."

Malcolm took the glass of brandy she'd poured for him, laughed and drank it in one swallow.

"Here's to tonight," he said.

As she took a sip, Callie held her glass to her lips for a moment and simply watched him.

As she started out, she glanced around to make sure they weren't leaving the room a wreck. Only his clothes lay untidily about where he had dropped them. The bed, neatly made by Consuela, had not been touched. Callie picked up Malcolm's clothes, surprised at how really soaked they were—his tuxedo jacket and trousers were heavy with rainwater, even his shirt and undershirt were soaked through. She could have wrung water out of his socks; bits of debris were stuck in them. He must have fallen down in the rain, she thought. But he was all right now and Callie had too much to do herself to worry about it. She quickly spread his dripping clothes over the back of a chair on her way out.

She couldn't tell how many minutes passed.

She took a little longer than necessary in the bathroom. When he walked into her bedroom, Callie was standing barefoot in white panties and bra. "You're staring at me," she said.

"You're beautiful."

"You just think I have a pretty rear end."

She felt a kiss on her mouth, a sweet kiss but not like the one he had given her at the end of the ceremony. "You're perfect all over," he said quietly.

"I feel a little shy of you now," Callie told him. "I never was before."

And then he looked at her in that way of his, drawing her toward him and making her want to cradle him. Tall, dark, a little disreputable-looking, comfortably leaning back against the bedpost with an unlit cigarette in his mouth, his legs crossed at the ankles, in light-gray trousers, a white shirt open at the collar and a navy blazer. Tranquil rain was falling on the roof. "I think I'd better wait outside," he said.

"Don't be silly. Stay here," she said. "We don't have to do that kind of thing anymore," and she reached out and took hold of his arm, but someone was knocking at the bedroom door. "Ah," Callie said, "there's Dorothy now," and threw on a robe.

But it was Consuela edging through the door, a tray containing a single tall glass of ice water in her hands. "I thought you were Mrs. Hudson," Callie said, disappointed. "Do you know what's keeping her?"

"No, Miss McKenna. I was all over looking for her."

"That's fine then. Just put the tray over there," Callie told her, indicating the top of the dresser. "That's all, thank you." Malcolm, she noticed, had gone over to the window and was studying the night. He put his hands on his hips, then impatiently looked at his watch. "It's about to stop raining," he said as if to himself. "That's good."

The maid left the tray and retreated.

Callie took a drink of water and dressed quickly. She wore a perfectly tailored Armani suit in a brown-pink crepe de chine. The outfit looked as she had meant it to do. It defined her figure softly, classically. She was about ready. She ran a comb through her hair and freshened her lipstick, then drew back to examine herself in the full-length mirror.

Callie realized she was lingering in the middle of this room where there was nothing more for her to do and her throat constricted with emotion, because now a part of her life had come to an end. She had promised herself that this wouldn't be good-bye, that soon she would come back to this same room and that—Oh, I don't know, she thought, I don't know. With a silent toast, she drained the cognac she had poured for herself and it burned all the way down her throat. It made her eyes water. She turned, picked up her purse from the side of the bed and went out.

Malcolm was waiting for her in the upstairs corridor. He made no effort to hid his impatience. He was walking up and down, smoking a cigarette, pulling hard at it in agitation. Flecks of ash had fallen on the front of his shirt.

"What makes you so restless this evening?"

He said he didn't know he was. "I guess I just want us to be on our way." He put out his cigarette, looked down at his hands, then smoothed his clothes, mechanically, fastidiously.

Callie wasn't about to let anything upset her tonight, or extinguish the tender flame kindled within her. Not tonight, she told herself.

He reached out and took her hand. "Callie, come here. It's you and me now. I'm so proud of you." The praise, the smile, the camaraderie embraced her. "What were you going to say?" he asked.

"Nothing."

"You were . . . I know you were."

"But now it doesn't matter."

There was nothing wrong at all. She had let her imagination get away with her, but nothing was wrong, was it? Nothing.

All at once, quite nervously, she ran her fingers up under the lapels of his jacket. She felt so shy she couldn't look at him, could only stare at her hands as she drew them slowly up and down. "Oh, my God, hold me!" she said, pressing her face against him. "Hold me, just hold me, will you?—for a minute, please—" She started to laugh at herself and burst into tears instead. The tears came as a surprise to both of them, but more to her than to Malcolm, she thought. He did as she asked; he put his arms around her and held her and let her cry telling her it was all right, everything was all right, go ahead, go ahead and cry, most natural thing in the world. Callie was ashamed of her weakness but she couldn't help herself. The minutes were delicate, as if they shared a secret too fragile for words.

They went back downstairs to the reception to say good-bye to everyone. And yet, in spite of Malcolm's impatience, it was another half hour of last-minute handshakes and kisses before they could stage their escape. Callie stood on the stairs and tossed her bouquet and it made a perfect long arc into Kristen's hands. "My fourth," she laughed. "It'll be my lucky number four."

At eight-fifteen a decoy limousine with a slip of wedding gown caught in the door sped toward the gatehouse and two security cars swung into line behind it. As the small motorcade shot past the gate, a barrage of flashbulbs appeared from nowhere, crackling in the night.

That should do the trick, Callie thought, and allow them to depart in peace. But instead of feeling relieved, she was beginning to feel more and more anxious. A maid came into the room with a tray of cocktails and canapés. "I was wondering," Callie said, "where Mrs. Hudson has gone—"

"I haven't seen Mrs. Hudson for . . . since it started to rain. I think someone said they left."

Uncertainty ran through Callie. "Are you sure? I knew they were leaving, but . . . this early? I'd hoped . . ." She looked around at the remaining guests and it seemed to her that they regarded her expectantly, even while they continued to talk to each other.

"All right, thank you," she dismissed the maid.

Callie took a glass of champagne and strolled, with studied indifference, to the living room. When she entered the open archway, a woman was laughing a low pleased laugh as if someone had made an indecent pass. Callie crossed the foyer to the opposite doorway and looked at a group of women seated facing each other on the twin sofas. Dorothy Hudson was not among them. She looked for her, searching slowly and deliberately through the length of the entire house. Dorothy and Emery must have already left for their holiday.

The rain had stopped. Through the window the lake glimmered between the boughs in mother-of-pearl strips. She looked out at the sky. It had cleared completely and was rich with stars like an immense night-blooming tree.

"Callie?" Malcolm took her arm. "Come on. Come on, if you're coming. Let's go."

All at once, Callie didn't want to see anyone—she had eyes only for him.

"I hope you'll come visit when you get back," Kristen was telling Malcolm. "We're just north of San Francisco."

"We'd be delighted to come. You'll be first on our list," Malcolm said.

"Promise?"

"Yes, I said so, didn't I? Of course."

"And Callie, what do you say?"

"I say . . . whatever Malcolm says."

The bride and the groom walked out into the night, a warm foggy August night that smelled of summer rain. A fragrant old path wound down through towering cedar trees to the boathouse. Followed by raucous celebrants, they hurried in silence, their footsteps whispering against the grass where it grew between the bricks. Malcolm bent his head beneath a low-hanging branch—the same branch where he had lowered his head many times before during their brief courtship—and let her go by.

In the shadow of the trees the lake was black; farther out beyond the shadows, it was quicksilver. Fog coiled up from the water like wisps of smoke. They rushed past the cove where the old dock still stood, the wood rotted and falling through, the bank now overgrown with cattails and lilies, buds thrusting above the water like serpent heads, some exploded open in red-throated plumage. No one noticed how the rushes were torn and strewn about, no one, including Callie, looked close enough to see the broken, crushed blossoms floating silently among the reeds. Ten feet farther along and up a ramp, the launch awaited them—the launch that would take them across the water to her car.

Malcolm assisted her on-board, both of them smiling and waving their good-byes as they went. Then, amidst a flurry of confetti and rice, Malcolm signaled the pilot and they pulled away into the main channel, still waving, the few remaining guests crowded onto the new pier to bid them farewell.

Behind them, the company of friends turned happily back toward the mansion, remarking among themselves what a fortunate young couple they were with their entire lives before them. Wind breathed in the rain-filled trees. Branches slowly tossed. And the night folded over the sound of their voices and footsteps and faded away.

In the cove, the ebb of the water was thick with floating shoals and eddies of confetti.

The minutes went trickling by.

Till all was quiet.

There was not much blood by then. And what little stain was left in the water after nearly two hours of rain, the darkness now obscured among the water lilies. No one had seen the faces of Emery and Dorothy Hudson that floated and nodded in the murky night-water of the cove. Held below the surface, with chains from the old railing around their shoulders like monstrous shawls, no one could have seen their eyes staring, hair undulating, soft and lazy like smoke, mouths parted in soundless screams, great, long, silencing slits torn in their throats.

Wedding Night
Santa Marengo

4

It was her new car they were taking, a midnight black Mercedes-Benz 500 SL, the car she had driven in *Blackspell.* The Hudsons had made her a surprise gift of the car when the picture came in under budget and on time. "Call it a bonus," Emery had said.

He was delighted when she was immediately pulled over for speeding, driving 80 miles an hour along a restricted stretch of the Pacific Highway. Callie McKenna, who always drove with such elaborate care! And to make matters worse, she burst into tears and offered the patrolman a twenty to let her go, "I'm really running late," she'd insisted. When he said, "I didn't hear that, Miss," she repeated her offer, loudly, so that he threatened to arrest her on a second charge of bribery. "I couldn't believe he was so dense," she complained while Emery howled with laughter. That was only a few days before she told them privately that she was getting married—but now it all seemed so long ago.

This evening when they opened the garage where the Mercedes had been hidden for the last thirty-six hours, they found it hadn't been touched. No tin cans or old shoes tied to the bumper, nothing scrawled in white tempera on the hood and trunk. "Perfect," she murmured and dangled the keys. "You drive."

While Malcolm checked their luggage, which was already stored in the trunk, Callie ambled around to the passenger side and got in. She thought it was risky for them to be driving such an expensive car; it was too recognizable and would only attract unwelcome attention. But when she had told Malcolm of her fears, he wouldn't take no for an answer. He couldn't wait to get behind the wheel again—so how could she say no? Callie was convinced that he had even changed their itinerary so they would spend part of it driving.

The door seemed to close on her by itself; everything around her was rich red leather and glittering chrome. She turned her head and took a last look across the lake. Against the blue-black sky, the lights in the Hudsons' windows were burning deeper and deeper, like forgotten campfires among the trees. She felt the finality of someone who was leaving her home for the unknown as Malcolm slid behind the wheel —her accomplice, her lover. She was still so much more a bride than a wife that she couldn't quite think of him as her husband.

The motor was running; he let the clutch out smoothly. He drove fast with the top down, both of them breathing the rough, damp air. "Not a minute too soon," he said, with a grin.

When they left the county road and swung up onto the interstate, they flew by too quickly to notice the flare of headlights behind them or the dark car that pulled out after them.

The night was sultry; they were tired; the moonlight flickered over their faces. Callie had never been so happy. She loved being next to him in the car. It was good to be moving, at last, away from the crowd and the noise—and to be alone. It gave her an exhilarating sense of adventure, of physical lightness, the two of them setting off into an immense new world of promise.

"Now you can tell me," she said. "Where are you taking me?"

"You'll see."

She smiled. "Okay, surprise me. I don't want to know."

Once Lake Arrowhead was behind them, all restrictions were off, all decorum thrown to the wind. There was no need to hurry, she reminded him, they were on their honeymoon; they had freedom measurable only in the depth of the stars. Malcolm drove west along the southernmost edge of the San Gabriel Mountains, through Pasadena, Glendale and Thousand Oaks. She lit his cigarettes for him, sometimes taking them back so she could taste the smoke he was tasting. She liked it when he was forced to slow down and stop at stoplights, because he would kiss her and slide his hand up between her legs.

They passed a car just as they reached the turnoff for Ventura, forcing them onto Route 192 instead of the interstate. But she would have wanted to take it anyway. I'm free, she thought. Free of the fickle public, the legions of photographers and reporters. How sweet the night was; sweet the moon on her face, sweet the warm night breeze that caressed her in an endless stream.

Gradually her tension dissolved and she realized she was ravenous. She was going to have something expensive to eat—whatever the hotel's specialty was.

"Did you book a table for dinner?"

"Of course."

"We're going to be too late," she said.

"They'll always stay open for you."

"You didn't give them my name, did you?"

"What do you think?"

Callie smiled. She was feeling more and more subdued, after the exhausting day. The car seemed to be going incredibly fast. Malcolm was humming a little tune she had heard before but couldn't place. With her head leaning against the back of the headrest, she was still adrift on the waters of the beautiful afternoon, swaying to the movement of the car. "Kristen claims she never met you at Michigan."

"Oh, yeah?"

"Yes. But, Mal, darling, she's always stirring up trouble. I know you were there. It's just something she said."

"Well, I was," Malcolm said. "I'll prove it to you."

"But you don't have to prove anything to me."

"Do you remember reading for a play? I think it was Shakespeare. They held it in that old auditorium right off campus. Does any of this ring a bell?"

"I don't know. Not really."

"I remember you holding out your arm —something about blue blood. No, blue veins."

Callie shifted on her seat and faced him. "Yes, I do remember that!" she said, excitedly. " *'My bluest veins to kiss.'* I do remember! Good grief, what made you think of that? I was trying out for Cleopatra. I still remember it. Let's see—*'With thy sharp teeth this knot intrinsicate . . . Of life at once untie. Poor venomous fool, be angry and dispatch . . .'* "

"Yes, that's it," Malcolm concurred, "but that's toward the end. You started your reading with something else. I'd remember it if I heard it . . ."

"I know what you're talking about. Let me think. *'The barge she sat in, like a burnished throne . . . burned on the water;*

the poop was beaten gold . . . Purple the sails, and so perfumed, that the wind was love-sick with them; the oars were silver . . . Which to the tune of flutes kept stroke, and made the water which they beat to follow faster . . .' " When she looked over at him, Malcolm was reciting the passage with her, word for word. He had known it all along. And when she stopped, he stopped and turned to her and laughed.

"That's the day I fell in love with you," he said. "I couldn't help myself. The whole room was in love with you."

She reached over and ran her hand over his cheek. He was telling her he remembered the first time he had seen her appearing in a movie and how he hated for the houselights to go on. The supple Mercedes took a long hill. And he was telling her how he dreaded leaving that luminous world to face a drab daylight where no one could ever compare to her.

"But, darling," she said, "that's only a dream world, a fabrication."

"Yeah. Ain't it a shame?"

Callie smiled. It was touching, she thought, that he would remember Cleopatra's lines all these years simply because she had spoken them. She wished she could remember as much about him.

The downside of the hill was steep and winding. Callie forced herself to stop trying to think and settled back to watch the headlights and the taillights go swimming past until it all became a soft blur.

Santa Marengo. Flowers. A boulevard running along a floodlit beach, sand the color of sugar-cinnamon. With a turn of the wheel, the Mercedes dropped between white balconied houses and they could see the black moonlit glitter of the Pacific. In their headlight beams, the hotel with bougainvillaea spilling from its terraces loomed before them. *Casa Del Mar.*

Callie took off the scarf she had put on when they'd started and folded it carefully. It was a Hermés scarf she had bought in New York last year while there on location, the day she got the telephone call informing her that her mother was gravely ill. She kept it with her now almost all the time.

The moon had come out, gleaming softly on the black car. Malcolm hit the accelerator once hard before he cut the engine. The evening sounds, the crickets, the clang of a distant buoy, settled over them. By then a liveried bellman was moving around the car toward her.

Nearly a half block behind them, the headlights went out on the car that had been following them as it rolled to the curb. With a twist of his fingers, Harwood turned off the ignition. He watched through the windshield as the bellman opened the car door for the bride; another stood at the trunk ready to collect the luggage. The girl swung her legs out onto the pavement, smooth and sleek. Completely unaware of the danger she's in, Harwood thought. After a moment, Malcolm got out, tipped the bell-men and spoke to him for a moment, giving him instructions. I've got to be careful, Harwood thought and slumped down, preparing to wait. She doesn't know. Malcolm hasn't told her anything.

Callie listened to Malcolm telling the bellmen which suitcases to bring up and then heard him say, "We'd like the car available day or night," but she couldn't decipher what else was said. When the four of them went in, she walked demurely beside her husband, taking his arm.

The lobby was old and ornate with

marble supporting columns and huge brass tubs of palms strategically located. A grand staircase curved up behind the main desk; a sense of decorum pervaded the vast open space. While Malcolm signed them in, Callie toyed unconsciously with a pen she had picked up from the counter, twirling the staff between her thumb and forefinger. The movement must have distracted him because without stopping what he was doing, he placed a firm left hand on her wrist and held it there with a gentle pressure that was almost fatherly. She took a few tentative steps toward the lighted terrace. Through an archway, she could see a few late diners seated at tables.

The clerk behind the counter told Malcolm the number of their reserved suite and handed the bell captain their key and looked at Callie with subtle recognition.

Malcolm came up behind her and slowly let his arms go round her; she saw herself in his arms reflected in a pier mirror: tall, tired, a little disheveled from the wind, but still, she thought with a smile, not bad looking.

In the elevator she said, "Let's not unpack. Let's just get ready and go down to dinner."

He followed her into a big sitting room with open curtains. A porter in a white uniform like a midshipman was at their heels bringing their luggage. In the adjoining bedroom stood a canopied relic of a bed, like a huge ship. The carved fronts of the armoire, the dresser and chest of drawers gave off a soft luster that seemed to move as she moved around them.

She pulled back the coverlet and ran her hand over the pillow. The white, taut sheets seemed the most wonderful luxury in the world. She caressed them with her hands before she turned on the light. The bed so beautifully turned down, so ready to take them in. Caught up in an illusion of being there with him, she wanted all of a sudden to forgo dinner, to call him to come lie down. Without touching him, she could almost experience the feel of his skin, the taste and smell of it like the smell of rain in the air before it actually arrives.

Malcolm gave the man a tip and asked him to hold their reservations in the dining room. They would be down in fifteen minutes. Once he had gone, she caught Malcolm's arm and drew him into the room, closing the door behind them, closing them together. "Well!" he said, wriggling his eyebrows roguishly.

"How long will we be staying here?"

"Tonight and maybe tomorrow night—at the most."

He was looking right at Callie now, bending over slightly, his eyes lit with tender sparks. When he stood too close to her, she sometimes lost the thread of what she wanted to say.

The porter had brought in her suitcase and her overnight case. Kicking off her shoes, Callie took the overnight case into the bathroom and opened it beside the basin, taking out her comb and brush, toothbrush and lipstick, a white silk wraparound nightgown. She brushed her teeth and lightly mended her face and lifting her head in a youthful, impatient movement, she tossed her red-gold hair back over her shoulder. She decided she would be overdoing it if she changed her clothes and went back to the bedroom. The rug felt wonderfully soft under her bare feet as she stepped into her heels.

She walked out on the balcony where

he was waiting. It was a beautiful evening, cool and damp, the sky like black velvet shot with stars. When she took his hand, she shivered, holding his fingers hard.

Quietly, he said, "Are you frightened?"

"Yes, a little, I guess . . ."

His eyes were watching her now. "Frightened of me . . ."

"No. Not of you. Everything seems so new." She held on to his strong fingers till hers were in pain. He grinned: it was that look of his that always drew her in. He took her in his arms. "We don't have to go down," he said into her hair. "You know, Callie . . . it's been a long time since we've been together."

"But I want it to go slow . . . everything slow from now on."

"I want everything to be perfect," he said and kissed her.

Among the potted palms on the courtyard below, a shadow moved unseen. There they are, Harwood thought, as they embraced on the balcony.

Halfway to the door, she stopped and turned. Malcolm was not watching her; he was looking out, standing rigidly, hands sunk in his jacket pockets. Callie lifted her hand out toward him. "Aren't you coming, Malcolm?"

Dinner was on the terrace, beneath the flowering trees.

They sat under the ivy-covered pergola, while silver lids were removed and course after course was presented and savored. Curried crab in endive spears. Breast of pheasant in a morel and sherry sauce. Wild mushroom pie. Dom Pérignon '78. Chocolate soufflé made of the thinnest air.

Minute by minute the spell grew on Callie until it was hard to recall the old world where she had dined with directors and agents and producers, where her name in letters thirty feet high commanded the night. Excellent as the food was, she found that she wasn't hungry after all. She sat at the table, digging her spoon into a chilled melon and sipping a glass of the champagne. Malcolm, on the other hand, ate ravenously.

"Callie, what's the matter? Aren't you going to have anything else?

"I couldn't. I'm not very hungry, that's all. This has been an emotional day. I'll get my second wind in a minute." She picked up her knife and fork. But her throat seemed actually to be closing.

Malcolm watched her. He said, "Don't. Not just to please me. You don't really want anything else, do you, Callie?"

It seemed to her then that she had loved him always, from the day she had first caught sight of him. With the soft constriction in her throat, she said, "Please kiss me."

He motioned for her to lean forward. She obeyed. Malcolm leaned over the corner of the table and kissed her very gently. When they drew apart, she couldn't answer for a moment. Then, still with that surprising constriction in her throat, she murmured, "No . . . that's all I want."

They made their way out of the deserted dining room.

It was difficult going back to their room, walking the few paces from the elevator to the door. And then going inside, locking the door, with him leading the way and Callie following. It was such freighted time, swollen with expectation and yet deliciously prolonged.

He drew the curtains and the bedroom was plunged into near darkness. Only a little light entered from outside through the shutters, printing in definite lines high on the wall and ceiling. The smooth grayness was now filled with even darker slow-moving shadows.

She lowered her head and stood perfectly still, holding her breath. Her heart was thumping. She spoke his name, hardly above a whisper: "Malcolm."

His arms tightened around her waist, knowingly, without haste, a slow, sensual motion that drew them together, and she submitted without moving, her eyes half shut, her body pressed close against him. He said, "Oh . . . you are exquisite."

She pulled his face to hers and kissed him open-mouthed and wetly. His lips were soft and strangely cool; his hands were on her skin and weaving through her hair. He had loosened her hair and it was tumbling all over her face and shoulders. He must have felt her pleading breath against his skin and her heart beating, must have been aware of her eyelashes closing over with pleasure. Her eyelids tightly shut, Callie permitted her clothes to be undone and lowered, then the straps of her slip and her bra, her naked breasts collapsing with his touch. She bent over him and offered him her lips.

He kissed her and then his hand passed slowly over the curve of her abdomen and when he laid his hand gently on the soft mound between her legs, her breath caught and she arched upwards, willing him to press harder. Her blood was beating heavily through her like a large vibrating drum and she was reaching up to him with her mouth. Her mouth was soft, feverish. Callie bit his tongue gently.

He touched her thighs, inching the skirt higher, then a little higher, until Callie gripped the bottom hem and lifted it up so that his hand lay on her skin. They stood like that for a moment, Callie aching for his hand to go on, and then Malcolm spread his fingers back over her hips and dug them gently in, and then harder and he was starting to rock her forward against him when Callie moaned, her skirt still caught in one hand.

"Close your eyes," he said.

"Why?" she murmured.

"Close your eyes, Callie. Close them. I won't hurt you. Promise."

Callie closed her eyes obediently. Her

panties were drawn down around her ankles and she kicked them off.

On his knees before her, under the drape of her lifted skirt as she stood, legs slightly spread apart, a bride of only a few hours, her eyes still shut as he kissed her there and she whimpered when he bit her with bites that were gentle and he sucked her, and she remembered saying, or trying to say, "Oh, you're . . . oh, Mal, don't stop . . ." but her voice had faded to silence. Her back was arched, her shoulder blades pressed against the wall, her fingers were in his hair, running through it and drawing into fists, guiding his head until without willing it she began to move with him, losing at last her need of slowness.

She drew a short breath, held it in her throat, let it out and again caught a breath and held it, held it until she couldn't any longer, and bending over him in a daze of ecstacy, her legs trembling, a thread of saliva suspended from her mouth, which she wiped away unaware with the back of her hand, she shaped the words, *Oh, there,* under her breath and followed it by saying, "It's wonderful this way," but she didn't even know if she said it out loud, or just thought she said it. *My God!* and Malcolm under there touching her all over, soft and slow like a cat's tongue. *God, I never knew a mouth could do so much.*

She felt her skirt loosened and pulled away. Even as he stood and reached out for her, the last of her clothes fell away and there was only the faint tinted luster of their naked bodies. And then he had lifted her in his arms and sank down with her on the bed. She felt the coolness of the taut sheets, his mouth. She whimpered when they kissed and her body gave itself; it opened to him and he came into her, slowly at first. She began to move her body in rhythm with his.

Then she murmured softly against his shoulders, "Hurry. I can't wait much longer," and what happened next was a blur to her, a whirl of pure animal hardness and moans and stroke after stroke and sweat and licking her everywhere and she was ready. She strained against him, murmuring, hungrily seeking his mouth again, wanting to cry out and unable to or to give more than a sound in her throat as if she were in mounting pain.

Her body rippled and rose against him

in hard, short furious waves. No longer thinking in words, she was all sensation and love. Groaning for breath, bodies like liquid fire moving without thought, pleasure, pleasure so close to pain, almost . . . almost . . . a little more, a little longer. Suddenly every muscle in her body seemed to lock, every one except for the slow grinding rotation of that one place, her head arched back, her breathing stopped, and the sweet fire shot through her nerves and consumed her entire body and then she began to cry out and she slammed her whole weight forward at the hip, thrashing her head back and forth and she came. Her cry of love slowly strangled back into a long, deep moan. She came again. She felt her senses erupt and away she was wafted—away, away. Because he was coming . . . because he was coming . . . because . . . coming under him, Christ coming, every time out of some deeper and deeper part of her, she reached a sensation far beyond frenzy, gone before she could capture it.

Her arms fell against her sides, her body slick. She was still in a world of spinning blood when she came to herself on the silken coverlet and dragged herself forward to kiss his spent and beautiful mouth. Then, gasping for breath, her mouth opened wide, she swallowed heaving mouthfuls of air.

"Malcolm," Callie muttered, reviving a bit, drawing herself softly against his damp length and laying her head on his chest, "please . . ."

"Yes."

"Kiss me again. Kiss me again or I'll die."

Before he could speak she leaned over him, brushing her mouth against his with a surprising, delicate tenderness and the curve of her body against his. "Oh, Mal," she said, "I'm so hot."

Even after, they could not stop. He pulled her gently farther down, closer to his waiting mouth.

An indefinable period of time passed while they lay there motionless; in the end she felt him take his hands away and struggle sideways until he could get out of bed. He stood and ran his hands through his hair. "I've got to cool down," he said quietly, pulling on his shorts.

He went to the sliding glass door to the balcony and opened it soundlessly. He stood there, looking out. The cool air entered the room. That's better, she thought, much better. She could hear the lapping of the waves in the distance. Little by little she realized that Malcolm wasn't just looking; he seemed to be watching, studying the night like an animal at the entrance to its cave. She saw nothing wrong in that; it made her feel protected. Guarded and safe.

"Don't you think," he said lovingly when he came back, "that we should try to get a few minutes' sleep?"

She rubbed her cheek against his hair. "No," she whispered. "You sleep. I'm still too worked up. All I want to do is lie here beside you for a while."

His head dropped heavily to the pillow and some minutes later he was asleep in Callie's arms.

Lifting herself on her elbow, she watched him sleep in dead peace. She wanted to lightly run her finger over the strong deep set of his eye with its tender curve of lid, touch his fine temple, the paleness of his forehead against the silky black shoots of his hair. His sleeping breath measured off the passing moments. This was how his body looked after it had left hers. She thought, If I woke him now, he would stretch out his arms and grunt like a lovely young animal.

Somewhere out in the warm, dark night, a bell buoy gently mourned. Callie listened to the bell, her eyes on the shifting darkness of the room, one hand weightless on his hip. Carefully she managed to slip out of his arms.

Fifteen minutes later she had had a cool shower and was feeling fine. Before she flicked off the light in the bathroom, Callie glanced at her watch. 2:10. She turned out the bathroom light without disturbing him and padded across the room to close the sheer curtains. Not a breath of air stirred. Outside everything was drenched with dew; it shone in the moonlight in great glistening beads.

Everything was steeped in silence; it was beautiful, she thought. How good it was to be alive. She was where she wanted to be. When she made her way back to bed, the voice of the bell followed her like a faint, sweet requiem.

Later she kissed his back and shoulders, which were hard and rope-muscled and tanned by the sun. He was sleeping with his head on his right arm, but when

Callie slipped in beside him, he stirred and groaned. His hair was still damp; his eyelids were twitching. After a long time, he turned on his side away from her. She wanted to make love to him, but it seemed almost cruel to wake him.

Once she thought she saw the glow of a feeble light under the door in the morning hours, but she couldn't be certain. She knew what the mind conjured at that hour might not bear close scrutiny in the raw light of day. Once or twice she dreamed she heard the low laughter of girls, and the menacing voice of a man, although the voices vanished before she knew for sure.

Someone was walking around. Their noises were keeping her awake; Callie tried to concentrate on where they were coming from. It sounded almost as though it were coming from the room next door, but it couldn't be. It had to be from the hall. She pushed off the covers and walked through the living room to the front door, opening it slowly. She looked out into the narrow hallway. No one there. She stood listening for a moment. The sound had stopped, but as Callie started to close the door she thought she heard the steps again. She pulled the door open abruptly this time, but again nothing was to be seen except the empty hallway.

Twenty feet away at the stairway exit, she noticed a cigarette burning in the ashtray, smoke curling in the air, and she wondered if someone was standing there behind the exit door. But she couldn't bring herself to go check it. She closed the door resolutely and stood there a moment, listening. The suite was intensely quiet—faint rustlings and creakings, perhaps settling floorboards—but quiet.

She went back to bed. When the footsteps started again, she merely lifted her head and listened. Slow steps. She couldn't tell where they were coming from. To prove to herself that she was responding to the power of suggestion, magnifying ordinary noises into something sinister and alien, she made a conscious effort to shake off the immobility of the moment before, going so far as to stretch, shake out her arms and legs and yawn. Then she got out of bed. Cautiously, she walked to the doorway between the two rooms, looking across the living room at the door—the shuttered door with the thin lines of light demarking each slat. And the shadow broke the horizontal lines—the outline of a man.

She stumbled back to bed, crawled under the covers and began to rock Malcolm's shoulder back and forth. He mumbled, sound asleep. She tugged harder and after a moment looked back over her shoulder, as if to fix in memory what she had seen a moment ago. But the shadows had vanished in the dull filtering light from the hall.

It was nothing; maybe she imagined it. Or dreamed it. She let her hand fall from his shoulder. There was no longer any reason to awaken him. No shadows. No dark outline. Callie sank back.

Even after her eyes were aching and heavy, she couldn't keep them closed. Callie sighed, thumped her pillow, then listened. Someone was moving about. I'm tired, she muttered to herself. I don't know what I'm thinking or feeling. Her eyes moved from the open window with its silent swaying curtain to the bedroom door, which stood ajar, back and forth, back and forth. I don't know what I'm thinking, she repeated dully. The curtain blew inward, until it stood in the air in a wide horizontal scallop.

She felt as if she woke up every five minutes all night long, but it might have been simply that she kept her lips touching him in her sleep, so that she knew he was there.

Once, half asleep, Callie remembered his saying, "You're mine now."

"Yes," she answered.

"Only mine?"

"Yes."

"You're mine now. You belong to me. Don't you?"

"Yes, yes. Oh, darling, for as long as I live."

Day Two—Sunday Morning
Casa Del Mar Hotel

5

The handgun was a 9-mm Beretta.

Harwood sat on the side of the bed cleaning it. He worked meticulously, using fine machine oil on a soft, white cloth from the kit in his suitcase. Dawn was breaking. Dove-colored light crept into the room on a breeze that smelled of dampness, of morning. In the glow of the bedside lamp, he wiped the gun down and then immediately removed the excess oil with a hand towel. From time to time he lifted his head and looked out through the sliding glass door, which he'd left half open. His binoculars sat on the nightstand.

With a thin strip of cloth, he cleaned the interior of the barrel. He released the clip and dropped it into his left hand, then emptied it of its cartridges. He held the Beretta up at arm's length, squinted through the leveled sights and squeezed the trigger.

The hammer struck with a hollow, metallic *clack.*

Satisfied, Harwood wiped the clip quickly with the oily cloth, reloaded it and snapped it into place in the handle. Again his fingers curled round the grained, ebony handles and he leveled the sights. The gun's weight and balance suited him perfectly. It seemed odd now, that after years of practice, his aim had become almost secondary—the range would be very close.

Carefully, he laid the Beretta on the rumpled sheet and got to his feet, stretching his arms and the aching muscles in his shoulders. Entering the bathroom, he thoroughly washed the traces of oil from his hands and then after tossing hot water on his face and smoothing on lather, he shaved with precision.

Taking his business suit from the closet, his shoes from under the bed and a clean white shirt from his suitcase, he dressed routinely, all his movements mechanical. He traveled light, carrying only his briefcase and the one suitcase.

Ready to leave, he leaned over and took up the gun. He kept it with him now, all the time. This morning, he set the safety and slid the Beretta into his belt on his left side, within quick and easy reach. It wasn't that he expected—or even wanted—to be able to get off a shot in a crowded hotel or in any other public place, but the circumstances dictated that he have the gun with him, ready, at all times. He had no idea what Malcolm might try to do.

Three minutes later, placing his suitcase and the black briefcase side by side at the foot of the bed to pick up later, Harwood left the room.

The light of day was still filtering through the darkness and mist drifted where the ground was low. The curtains were drawn on all the surrounding windows; when he passed by number 19, he heard a muffled gust of laughter from an early morning television news show. None of the comforts the hotel offered could deter him for an instant from the task at hand.

Keeping away from the lobby, he went through an arched doorway lined with roses and oleander, crossed the drive and strolled down the sidewalk toward the outdoor parking lot. He looked back where the bellman was usually stationed, but no one was there. He didn't see anyone else, but he hurried all the same, not wanting to take any chances. The nearest streetlight, twenty yards away, was a yellow haze in the mist, and he skirted its light.

At this hour the gatehouse to the lot was unoccupied; a sign indicated that it would open at 6 A.M. Thirty-five minutes from now. PLEASE INQUIRE AT FRONT DESK, read a second placard. Harwood headed for the dark back row of the parking lot, where he saw the black gleam of the car Malcolm had been driving.

When he reached the shelter of a stand of trees, he stopped and looked back toward the hotel, even though he knew there was nothing to see. Wasting no time, he turned and walked the forty feet to the black Mercedes SL. As Harwood moved down its side, he ran his fingers over the expensive black paint of the hood, which was cool to the touch.

All at once on the other side of the fence, someone ran past him, right past him, no more than a couple yards away— startled, he bent down. What the hell was that? A jogger—he'd hardly caught a glimpse of him—running hard but with light steps in the direction of the neighboring resort.

When no one else appeared, Harwood straightened. That had shaken him, whoever it was—it must've been somebody out running for the hell of it. Shaken him to the core. He wondered if, in the mist, the runner had even seen him. At the rear wheel-well on the driver's side of the Mercedes, Harwood stooped down. From his jacket pockets, he took out a transmitter no larger than a deck of cards. He threw the switch to activate the transmitter's signal and reaching up under the chassis, attached it magnetically to a brace underneath the rear quarter panel. He tugged at it and it wouldn't budge. Now try to get away, he thought.

The sun floated through clouds in the east as he stood and walked away. He watched the sky lighten, and the trees and shrubs fill with dimension. The resort next door blazed with red fire as the sun struck its column of glass. Headed toward the gatehouse, he met the attendant who was just coming on duty.

"I've been looking for you," Harwood said. "Would you have my car brought around? In about an hour?" He kept walking. When he took the monitor from his breast pocket and tested it, the blue bead winked like a slow steady heartbeat. Just as it should.

At 6:15 when the dining room opened, he took a table by the window and ordered breakfast. And by seven o'clock, knowing he had to be patient, he had begun his vigil.

Malcolm opened his eyes. All his instincts were awake and on alert. He had been in trouble so often and for so long, he could smell it on the air like a scent. It was 10:15.

He got out of bed carefully, so as not to disturb Callie, and started to get dressed. Something was wrong. He pulled on boxers and sweats and his old Reeboks, then slid the room key and a couple of twenties into the slash pocket of his sweatshirt. As he strapped on his watch, he looked down at Callie's sleeping face, her copper hair spread on the pillow, a bare shoulder jutting above the sheet. She was so healthy and wholesome and fine. He wanted to protect her from all the hurts of the world. God only knew how much longer they would have and everything must be perfect now, in the little time they had left.

If she knew . . . he thought. If she knew about me. It would be over . . . everything ruined. But his mind couldn't conceive of it.

He was out there. Malcolm knew he mustn't think of his father, who could be very clever and convincing. He would be searching for him now, without any doubt. Rage boiled up in him. To go back to that. To be forced to go back to that. He felt uncontrollable rage and a horrible fear. Callie must never find out. Never.

The doctors had warned him that he could be his own worst enemy, that there'd be times when his fear would make traps for him, that there'd be a weakness in him that couldn't take the stress. But not this time. The feeling of danger was so strong that it made Malcolm glance behind him at the closed door and then around the suite. But there was nothing to see, of course. No one was there. He tried to dismiss the feeling, but he couldn't—something was happening out there. And there was no telling what trap had been set.

At the sliding glass doors that led to the balcony, he drew the sheer curtains aside and peered out, the smell of seaweed and salt in the air. Nothing unexpected met his gaze: cumulus clouds drifting through a blinding clear sky. The muffled sound of hotel life came to him as in a dream, easy and pleasant. Long ago he'd taught himself to filter and interpret even the smallest sound, becoming instantly alert at the first wrong note.

But this morning not even the slightest sound seemed out of place. On the terrace below, he listened to the waiters joking while they put up the white square-shaped umbrellas over the luncheon tables; he could even hear the manager calling out directions from inside the open-air dining room. Maids were making up the adjoining suite; one of them cleared away several clinking glasses. He heard distinctly the snap of a clean sheet in the air; in another room, a vacuum hummed briefly. The women's voices muttered and grumbled in Spanish—he thought it was—or maybe Portuguese. Then they faded away. Quiet, again. Nothing alarming. The smoke of a cigarette floated up in the air.

Again slowly he scanned the outer edges of the interior courtyard. His eyes stopped suddenly and returned to the open passageway leading out to the parking lot. Something was reflected on one of the large, boutique windows. Or was it? Yes, there it was again, a thin shadow almost un-noticeable. Without removing his eyes from it, he studied the featureless shape as it dis-appeared and came into view again.

It was a man.

Fear flashed through him. *Is that . . . ? Is that my father?*

Malcolm looked again. Impossible to tell who it was or whether the figure had anything at all to do with him. Is that him? *Find out.*

He ran his sweaty palms down the sides of his sweatpants. The man was, in fact, only visible when the breeze pressed against the windowpane and turned it dark and reflective.

Malcolm let the curtain fall shut and started for the door, but turned to take a last look around. The question, ever-pres-ent, ran through his mind: Will you be all right? Callie's breathing was slow and regu-lar and deep; it remained unruffled as he silently shut the door behind him. I'll be back before anything can happen, he thought. He tried the doorknob; the door was locked. He had to trust that Callie would be safe here for a little while. If he gets too close to her, he thought, I'll kill him. I'll have to kill him. I won't have any choice.

The corridor was empty; a few unsightly breakfast trays littered the carpet outside closed doors. Halfway down the hall he heard a click from somewhere and froze, poised to slip away. What was that? He waited and listened. No one was moving about. He ran his hands through his hair; he was drenched with sweat.

Now the silence was becoming unbearable. He hurried on toward the elevators, then abruptly changed his mind and ran down the three flights of stairs and outside.

Half dead with fear and rage, he took the path under the large umbrellas the waiters had erected, but by the time he had a clear view of the passageway, the figure was gone.

Where was he? Where had he gone?

He didn't pass me, Malcolm thought. He must've gone out on the street. Now he would have to search for him until he knew for certain who the man was.

● ● ●

Deep silence. She was alone. She knew it even before she opened her eyes. Callie lay quite still, and everything in her hung in careful suspension, like a big agile cat drowsing on the low branches of a tree. The night was still upon her. It glowed; it flickered in her veins. The new day had not penetrated her consciousness except as a scarlet blur staining her eyelids. She stayed that way for a long time, in a state of physical and mental limbo, on the threshold of sleep.

Slowly her eyes opened to slits, then a little wider. A streak of sunlight was quivering on the ceiling and she could hear seagulls outside, the muffled crash of waves. She could smell the clean salt air. It was a morning of blazing sunshine, clear, bright, shimmering yellow. Mirrors and crystals caught the light, breaking it into brilliant splinters. Seeing the over-decorated room for the first time in daylight, she thought it had a look of pretty impermanence. Like an abandoned movie set.

She felt wasted. After a while, she peered over at her travel alarm. 10:50. How could it be so late? It didn't seem possible. Lifting her head, she saw her things strung across the floor by the bed, just as she had lost them, piece by piece, the night before. When she stirred, her skin felt almost raw against the sheet. It was like returning to consciousness from a high fever. Callie lay back on the bed, in the warm sheets, limp, naked, exhausted. There was something wonderfully private and casual and intimate about lying alone in the unmade wreckage of her wedding bed. She rolled over and sat up, yawning, and brushed the tawny mane of hair back from her face. Her bare breasts felt warm and heavy, and her nipples ached, sweetly. They were sore and tender as if delicately stung.

I'm like a chrysalis, she thought, tender and new. I've shed my old body. How long had it been since she had experienced a feeling of release like this? She felt no need of anything—no need to hurry, not the slightest weight upon her heart or mind.

When at last she did get out of bed, she stood experimentally, surprised at how well her legs remained under her. From outside came the rustling of palms and always the underlying stillness. Slipping the white gown around her body, Callie made her way to the large patio window that opened onto the balcony and, parting the sheer curtains, looked down through the treetops to the garden terrace below. Tied to no schedule, free of the frustrations and the pressures of the movie set, she wondered where Malcolm was now. Vaguely, she thought she remembered his saying he was going out, but she couldn't be sure. Maybe she had dreamed it. Anyway, she was used to it by now. She wasn't sure how long he had been gone, probably less than an hour.

The day always began earlier for Malcolm. He had warned her that he was an early riser; even as a boy he had had a paper route. What he really liked was to get up in the dark and begin the day before sunrise. When he was with her, he sometimes humored her by staying in bed until it was light, but then it was his habit to get up, throw on sweat clothes, and go for a run before breakfast. He said no matter how hot and polluted the day might become, early in the morning the air was cool and fresh and sparkling.

On her way to the bathroom she picked up the clothes that were lying on the carpet. She gathered up his trousers, shirt, and navy blazer. Finally she had to admit to herself that today, of all days, it was a disappointment to awaken and find him gone. Still she wasn't going to make a big production out of it.

Through the fabric, she felt his wallet in one of the hip pockets, and she had the unusual impulse to look through it, but she dismissed it. What sort of woman went rummaging through her husband's things anyway? Callie did remove the wallet, though, along with his change and the folded bills from his front pocket and left it all piled on the bedside table, in order to properly hang up his trousers.

Speaking croakily into the telephone, she ordered a pot of black coffee and croissants, along with the morning papers. She asked how long it would take and was told it would only be a few minutes. Then with the door closed, Callie ran her bath. Except for faint shadows under her eyes, her face in the mirror did not show any signs of strain, and yesterday's sun had even given her some color.

She loved to pack and unpack, when she could take her time doing it. She had bought two new suitcases from Mark Cross, one a large utilitarian suitcase in calfskin, the other a neat white canvas with brown leather straps. Both bore her new initials: CMR. She held up her prettiest summer dresses and skirts, appraising them in front of the mirror. Then, lifting Malcolm's clothes affectionately from his suitcase, humming to herself, she remembered how he liked to have things done for him.

His white shirts of fine Egyptian cotton, even his old clothes—the worn brown belt with the engraved buckle, for instance— these were his things and she loved them. Callie had a joyful moment when she thought of their life together, years of doing things for each other, years of pleasure.

When the discreet knock came at her door, she went to take the tray from the waiter and had to remind herself to sign the bill with her new married name. "It looks like you forgot to bring my morning newspaper."

"I'm sorry," the waiter said. "But we have orders about that. From Mr. Rhodes. He said to let you rest; he didn't want anything disturbing you. Not even the newspaper."

She couldn't keep from smiling. "Oh, he did, did he?"

"Yes, Ma'am."

"All right. I'll need to speak with Mr. Rhodes. Never mind." She found the last two dollars in her purse, tipped him and closed the door.

Callie loved the aroma of dark roast coffee: she drank two cups with her croissant.

In the bathroom, she slipped out of her gown, once again aware of how taut her body looked emerging naked and smooth from the white silk. She lay back in the warm bath, resting her head against the rim, spreading luxurious soapsuds up and down her arms.

Malcolm delighted in laughing at her and calling her "a hopeless romantic," and although she always laughed with him and protested, Callie knew he was probably right. She tried to be cautious. And yet, in spite of her knowing air, she knew she was something of an innocent. Most of the time, she believed what people told her but she had to be constantly on guard; she knew sometimes she seemed to ask for it, playing the innocent girl, too good to be true. Well, she could hardly be accused of that any longer, she thought, not after last night, and smiled with a sudden increase of confidence.

She wanted the life she had never had. Wanted it all. The white picket fence, the husband who would be there for her, the three children. She hadn't told anyone yet, least of all Emery and Eddie Ketchum and certainly not Malcolm, but she was thinking seriously of giving up the role they were holding for her in *Transgression.* Malcolm would receive his degree in January. With the money they had set aside, they could live very well until he established himself. She might give it all up for a while—take a year off. It would be a dangerous—some would even say capricious—thing to do, considering the fickle nature of the business. Even as late as a month ago, she would never have believed she could be thinking like this. She had worked hard to get where she was and yet, every day, she found it harder and harder to believe in—as if at any minute it could all be taken from her.

It had been a daunting experience for an eighteen-year-old to quit the university without even finishing the first semester and set out to launch herself as an actress.

That first year in New York she'd landed the lead in Cass Cassidy's cult film, *Afterlife*. Beginner's luck, everyone said. But the next three years had been a waste, there was no denying that. She'd appeared in her share of dogs, a string of crime and horror movies, sometimes making as many as five a year and yet there were perilous times with no job at all and no money coming in. She was on a one-way street to the bottom when she met Emery and Dorothy, and her world changed.

The last few days, she could feel it changing again. Over and over, she felt herself left with the one certainty of her life that meant anything. She was married now—all the rest was shriveling behind her like black ashes.

Minutes later she was feeling fine. Wrapped in a thick terrycloth robe, her hair up in a towel, she'd had a long soak and was lying back on a pillowed chaise on the balcony. Again she wondered where Malcolm was, trying to stem her disappointment. In the weeks since their secret engagement, she had tried to accommodate his unannounced comings and goings. Sometimes he left messages for her, sometimes not. After a couple of minor arguments, he had promised to let her know if he was going to be gone for any length of time. Between her schedule and his, there were times when she hardly knew where he was. And this morning—the first morning of their life together—she missed him. She wanted him there.

Across the way, a huge tomcat stretched along a railing in the sun and eyed her with casual interest. Faraway, as if in some other dimension, a car door slammed. She leaned back in the chaise lounge, waving her hands before her in the air to dry the nail polish. Nothing but the monotonous waves striking the sand, as repetitive and effortless, it seemed, as slowly drawn breaths and somewhere far away, too distant to be annoying, the shrieks of children playing in the water.

She looked down at her toes, protruding a half inch from her sandals, and considered painting them too—luscious red-pink, like her fingers. But not yet. It was too much trouble to move. And there was plenty of time. Time stretched before her in an unwinding stream through the whole long, languorous day. She closed her eyes.

It was 11:25, the lazy lull before lunch with the long California afternoon still before them. The table on their balcony had been set for two while she had finished making herself presentable; a waiter would be arriving any minute now with their lunch. She couldn't help but wonder about Malcolm. Still, she knew he had taken the time to order their lunch the night before. *So where was he!* Obviously he planned on coming back in time to join her.

Below on the terrace, the first luncheon guests to arrive ordered Bloody Marys. She heard the words quite distinctly as if through a funnel and she opened her eyes long enough to see the tomcat, without seeming to hurry, slide from his perch and vanish into the underbrush. Lifting her arm so that the hand hung down, she brushed back a wisp of her hair with her wrist. This was peace. If only she could hold this moment for one more hour. But something warned her it wouldn't last. It couldn't; it was too perfect.

The tables on the terrace continued to fill up. Arriving by car, other luncheon guests mingled with those who were staying at the hotel. The maître d' was hard at work. A party of five in the far right corner. A party of two directly below. And now more noise, more conversation, more glasses tinkling and plates and silver clattering, so that the slow rhythmic splash of the Pacific, which had been so prevalent earlier, now seemed remote.

Promptly at 11:45, there was a tap at her door. When she opened it, a waiter greeted her and entered pushing a luncheon cart laden with silver serving dishes. Callie led him to the balcony, where she asked if he would just leave the cart and the serving pieces; she would serve them herself. Positioning the cart where she asked him to, the waiter bowed slightly. "As you wish," he said.

She had started toward her purse for a tip when she remembered the money she'd taken from Malcolm's trousers and left on the nightstand. No harm in her using it, she thought. Malcolm wouldn't mind.

The bills were folded in half like a book: three ones showing on the outside, a five and two twenties on the inside. She peeled off the ones and gave them to the waiter, who wished her, "Bon appétit and a pleasant afternoon," as a piece of blue paper fluttered to the floor. It must have been stuck between the bills, she thought. Automatically, the waiter stooped and retrieved it for her as she let him out.

Callie remained standing by the closed door, one hand still on the knob, the other holding the blue paper. She recognized it at once. It was a sheet of Emery Hudson's blue notepaper folded down to a one-inch square.

The memory rose in her mind like a photograph. Yesterday: the maid handing Malcolm a note and him reading it before following her through the French doors. Was this the same piece of paper? Today, around its edges, it showed dry water stains. She felt uneasy. She tried to shake the feeling, but couldn't. The note crackled as she unfolded it.

The handwriting scratched on it was undeniably Emery's even though the ink had bled badly, the words faint, barely legible. It read:

Malcolm,
Your father is here. Meet us
immediately in the boathouse.

Don't upset Callie. Leave her out
of this. Come by yourself. Now.
E.H.

Callie read it through a second time,
then a third and then she simply stared at it
in disbelief. Maybe if she could only look at
it long enough it would tell her more than it
said.
Malcolm's father! At the wedding?
It seemed utterly incredible. Why
hadn't she been told? Obviously there
must've been some mistake. Someone saying he was Malcolm's father in order to
crash the gate. But if that's all it was, why
didn't Malcolm just say so? Why all the se-
crecy?
Wandering back across the room, Callie folded the paper along its original
creases and slipped it into her pocket, but
after a moment she took it out again and
examined it thoroughly once more. How
could this be?
The paper had gotten wet. She remembered Malcolm suddenly appearing in the
Hudsons' upstairs hallway, his clothes
soaked through. If the note hadn't slipped
among his folded money, the ink would

have most likely dissolved; it would've been illegible, destroyed.

Where are you, Malcolm? she thought. Where are you now?

On the balcony, she looked down across the large central fountain, artfully arranged with potted azaleas and weeping figs. There was movement everywhere: people in an intermittent stream flowed below her over the tile. A well-dressed couple followed the maître d' through the maze of tables. White-coated waiters darted back and forth. He's down there somewhere, she thought. But there was only one man who did not move—a man half concealed behind a potted weeping fig tree.

Some trick of light on the surrounding glass surfaces all but blinded her. Callie snatched up her sunglasses, put them on and the dark lenses gave a deep tone to everything. The blazing white walls turned tawny, the ocean became purple, the red bougainvillaea took on a rich, burnished hue. Now that she could see him clearly, Callie realized that the man had been standing over there, his back to the wall, watching her, all this time.

The damned paparazzi.

She felt almost physically ill. *Oh, God, it's starting. Malcolm, where are you? Now we'll never get rid of them.* Her eyes searched every crack and crevice where a lens might be hidden to take her picture, but she saw nothing unusual. All at once it occurred to her that she was just standing there in plain sight and she stepped back into the shadows.

The blood drummed in her ears, made her feel giddy. The man down there wasn't attempting to photograph her—so he must be a reporter, she concluded, or a spotter. But how had he found them? It eventually dawned on her that she was not the only one the man was watching. He kept turning his head, looking down toward the beach through the wide breezeway—at what she couldn't tell. The air was still; even the leaves hung motionless on the trees. *Who are you?* Slowly the man's head rotated and he was gazing up at her again.

Although she could not see him clearly, even from this distance she could feel his eyes fixed on her. Callie stared back, but it did not cause him to falter. *How dare you!* she thought. *I'm going to demand that you knock it off.*

She grabbed her purse, rushed out of the room, the door closing behind her, and found herself alone in the deep, soundless heart of the hotel. She punched the button for the elevator repeatedly. When it didn't come, she turned and ran down the stairs, wondering what Malcolm would think when he found her gone.

She passed a couple on the stairs, but they stepped aside and didn't try to speak to her. The instant she reached the first floor she rushed out through the lobby, into the sunshine. Callie searched the terrace restaurant and finally caught a glimpse of the man. It lasted only a moment. Then he was gone, following the path around to the parking lot. She ran a few steps after him, but knew it was no use. She would never catch him.

She crossed the open terrace to the exact spot where the man had stood. As the luncheon guests passed by and the hot August sun beat down, she gazed up at the balcony where she herself had been standing only minutes before. Callie turned her head and looked down toward the beach as the man had done. And saw Malcolm—talking to one of the waiters. Then she saw that Malcolm was looking back at her.

She lifted her hand to wave, but she was suddenly aware that a freckle-faced teenage blonde was bearing down on her, squealing, "I know who you are! Is it really *you?*"

There were two of them: the other girl was a redhead with a heavy body and a high, nervous giggle. "We'd know you anywhere," she said. "Oh, my God! *It is you!* It's Callie McKenna! I can't believe it—it's really you!"

The only way for Callie to deal with the girls was to put on the best performance she could muster. She turned to them with a bright, unnatural smile.

"Could I ask you one thing?" the blonde was pleading. "Just one thing, would you mind taking off your shades? Shades—you know, your sunglasses?"

It took five long minutes for Callie to get rid of them, even after signing her name twice on pages of a small spiral notepad. As soon as they were gone, she looked for Malcolm again, but he had disappeared from the beach.

She raced back upstairs. Upon entering the suite, she saw that the door to the bedroom was ajar and through it she could see Malcolm darting about, collecting things, throwing them into suitcases. She heard him saying, "God! God! God!" under his breath. He stepped into the bathroom and returned, zipping his Dopp kit. Callie had never seen him like that before. She wasn't sure if he even noticed her standing there.

"Malcolm," she called to him, "there's someone watching us."

"I know." He was clearly in such a turmoil that he made no attempt to come to her. No attempt to kiss her.

"Did you see him?"

He hardly focused on her as she entered the room. And when he did, it was with an expression of aggravation, she thought. Or anger. "Yes," he said, "I saw him, too."

"I came downstairs . . ."

"Was he looking at you? How close did you see him?"

"Not close," Callie said, waiting for him to answer and then she went on, unhappily, "It's probably someone from the tabloids. If they've found us . . ." She stepped up to him and tried to put her arms around him, but Malcolm only half turned and, swiftly, lightly, kissed her on the corner of the mouth. He was in no mood for it, shrugging off her embrace, even though she tried to prolong it.

"Come on, Callie, let me go." He extricated himself from her. "Give me a hand; we've got to get the hell out of here."

Stung by his rejection, she swallowed the sudden lump in her throat and did as her husband asked. While she quickly finished putting their suitcases together, he was on the phone with the front desk, settling the charges with his credit card and telling them to bring the car around. She struggled with a growing sense of uneasiness, but kept telling herself they really had nothing to fear. Still she could feel *his* fear transferring to her.

The pained expression remained on his face as they went down in the elevator, she noticed. Tense as a steel spring, he leaned in the corner, ready to fly out the door as soon as they hit the lobby.

The black Mercedes sat under the canopy, waiting for them.

"Callie, hurry," he said, tossing their

bags into the trunk and getting behind the wheel. "Quick, come on, let's go." He dropped the gearshift into drive and they were off.

They sped down the avenue of palms, the sunlight flashing over them and the bells in steeples ringing Sunday morning mass.

"What's the matter, Malcolm? What is it?" she asked. "You're not in some kind of trouble, are you?"

His eyes seemed glazed with preoccupation. "No. No trouble."

"Then tell me what it is."

"I'm in no trouble—honest to God, I'm not in any trouble."

With an effort, she kept an outward appearance of calm—she was usually good at that. "What then?"

"I don't know—I'm living in a sort of hell," he said.

"What do you mean . . . It's only a reporter. Is this because of me?"

"No. No, Callie, it has nothing to do with you," he snapped. "Stop thinking the world revolves around you."

She came back at him. "But if it has to do with you, it has to do with me!"

Malcolm gripped the steering wheel

and stared straight ahead. Silent. And Callie felt utterly shut out. Alone. Hurt. *Stop thinking the world revolves around you.* She wanted to move away from him, but there was nowhere to go. She had slept with him, made love to him, shared moments of the most exquisite intimacy with him—and now she studied him as if she had never seen him before in her life. My world revolves around you, Callie thought. Unexpected tears filled her eyes.

What had happened to their glorious honeymoon?

Toward nightfall, reporters began calling the hotel. Word had gotten out that the actress, Callie McKenna, was married and that the bride and groom were staying there in the bridal suite. The hotel denied that they were there. As far as anyone knew, the couple had simply vanished into the countryside.

6

"**H**ow are you, my darling? Is everything all right?"

The bony hand trembled to press the receiver tighter to her ear. "Yes, oh . . ." For a moment, she could hardly speak. "Oh, thank God, it's you, Preston. I've been waiting and waiting. I though you'd never call."

"Everything's all right, sweetheart. Don't get excited. I told you I'd call, don't you remember?"

"Is Malcolm with you? Oh, say he is."

Silence. "Not right now, Evelyn."

"Have you seen him, Preston? I think about him all the time. I'm so afraid."

"Sh-h-h. Now don't get so worked up. I have to be careful. I can see his car from where I am right now. I'm looking out the window and I can see his car. That's how close I am."

"Then, why . . . Preston, why? Haven't you even talked to him?"

"You know why, Evelyn. We've been through this before. We've got to be careful. There's no other way."

Suddenly tears broke from her eyes and ran down her cheeks. "Can't you just bring him home?"

"Evelyn, I told you: it's not like that this time. He's married now. Don't you remember?"

"Oh, tell me about his girl, Preston. Is she pretty?"

"She's an actress," he said, quietly. "She doesn't know anything."

"Will you be bringing her, too?"

"That wouldn't be . . . that's not such a good idea."

Evelyn Harwood covered her mouth and sobbed. All of a sudden, she ripped her hand away and gasped out, "What are you going to do? What are you going to do to him? Can't you just bring him home, Preston? Can't you? He's our son!"

"Evelyn . . . Evelyn . . . Sweetheart . . . I won't lay a hand on him. It'll be just like it was the last time."

With her knees drawn up in the coverlet, she put her head down on her arm and the horror and the loneliness that had been waiting and gathering came flooding in and she wept. She felt utterly powerless and she hated it. She wept and wept, she didn't know how long. Finally she wiped her face and picked up the receiver where she had dropped it and said, "I'm sorry, Preston, I'm sorry. Don't be mad at me. I'm trying to be good. I'm doing everything just like you told me. All my pills. I'm trying to get better . . . so I can get out."

"Yes," he told her, "that's the thing to do. You'll be fine. Call downstairs and have Vivian come stay with you. I left strict instructions that you were to have the best of everything. Don't worry so much. And try to get a good night's sleep."

"Don't hang up, Preston . . . oh, Preston, promise me nothing bad will happen . . ." Then suddenly she whispered, *"Watch out for yourself!"*

"Don't worry about me," he said, soothingly. "I've got to go now. It's late and I'm dead tired. I'll call you soon."

"Okay," she answered, "bye-bye," and yet after the line went dead, she thrust the covers away, angrily, and got out of bed. *Watch out! Watch out! How could he? Her own flesh and blood.*

In her bare feet she began to roam desperately around the attic room. All at once she turned and ran to the dresser under the painted rafters, and opened the top drawer, throwing out bedclothes and underwear, running her thin fingers through everything that was in it. Not there. She pulled open the next drawer down, and again dug through stacks of sheets and pillowcases until her hands seized upon the photograph in the small, walnut frame.

Everything in her, the frenzy and panic, slowed. She ran her hand over it lovingly. It was the last picture of him remaining in the house. Years ago in a fit of anguish, Preston had destroyed all the others; she had only been able to ferret this one away and hide it. Her Malcolm, her own little boy. In the photograph he was not yet six years old. He stood next to his father, who towered over him and his little hand reached up to be swallowed in his father's hand. His face was so small, so delicate, no larger than the fingernail on her little finger. And yet it was him. It was his face. His beloved face. The dearest, tenderest, most innocent face in all the world.

Moonlight and shadows moved over the picture, the iron bars casting dark columns. Evelyn turned and made her way to the window and her fingers curled round the bars and she began to pull at them and shake them as if she could tear them apart.

A scream. A scream tore the night. Harsh and agonizing.

The shock of it almost threw Callie out of the bed. It froze her brain as if a blinding light had burst on her eyes. Then she realized it had come from Malcolm, right beside her.

Now he was moaning, "Don't do that. Don't. Don't do that."

She caught him by the shoulders, but he was slippery with sweat and she couldn't control him.

"Malcolm, *Mal!*"

As she drew nearer, she was certain that he said, "Get out! Gotta get out."

And yet when she smoothed his hair back from his forehead and said, "What is it, darling? Tell me," the muttering stopped entirely. All at once, he flung himself upright and awoke with a gasp, unable to stop the momentum of his nightmare. He choked, his staring eyes filled with fright.

When Callie touched his shoulder, she felt his muscles jump. "Darling?" The violence on his face unnerved her. She kissed his cheek, his hair. "I'm here," she said, "I'm here. Only me. It's only me. No one else."

He shuddered and fell back against the pillows, looking up at her blankly. She said, "God, Malcolm, what was that all about?"

He said nothing. Fully awake now, he began to free himself from her. "What time is it?" he asked. "How long was I asleep?" He was soaking wet with sweat.

"I don't know," she said. "It's . . . late." While she ran to the bathroom for a towel, he methodically went around the room, slammed the three windows shut, locked them and pulled the gingham curtains.

He had reached the open door—he was standing there intently studying the night by the time Callie came back and wiped his face with the towel and down across his chest. "Let's go to bed," she said, putting her arm around him and gently tugging at him, attempting to lead him away. But she couldn't; he was like a rock.

Even after the lights were out, he stood at one of the windows, the curtains barely parted, staring at the moonlit highway. I can't let her know, he thought. Can't let her find out. He's out there right now. Waiting. Waiting for me.

Behind him, he heard her beckon. "Come to bed, darling. Everything's okay."

All was quiet.

In number 11 at the Pinecrest Terrace across the highway, Harwood set his travel alarm and turned off the light. The bead of the electronic tracker winked beside him like a slow, sleepless, blue eye.

Day Three—Noon
The Sierra Nevada

7

Monday morning, 11:20.

They had stopped at a highway restaurant near Camp Nelson in the northern foothills of the Sierra Nevadas. Clint Black's "Put Yourself in My Shoes" was playing on the jukebox, the red-checked tablecloth had the smooth soft heft of a thousand washings, and the aroma of home cooking drifted from the kitchen. "I've got to ask you something," she said, "and you're not going to like it."

He chuckled. "Don't ask it then."

"I have to. It's making me crazy." She concentrated on speaking evenly, ignoring the pounding of her heart. "Tell me the truth . . . was your father at our wedding?"

Slowly his eyes gathered in a squint. "What?"

"Mal, I've got to know . . . did you see your father at our wedding?" Callie reached into her purse and held out the folded blue notepaper, watching for his re- action. His entire manner changed, a wari- ness settling over him.

"What's that?"

"When I went to pay the waiter at the hotel, it fell out of your pocket. I didn't know what it was, so naturally I looked at it. I think it's the note the maid gave you at the wed- ding. It's in Emery's handwriting. It says . . ."

"Let me look at that." Malcolm took the note, then looked over at her, steadily. "It also says not to upset you. Didn't you see that, too?"

"But why would you keep it from me?"

"Look, Callie, it unnerved me too, I'll admit. I went out to the boathouse, in the rain, but no one was there. Emery wasn't there . . . no one." As he spoke, Malcolm returned the notepaper to its folds and then, to her surprise, he tore it to shreds, deliberately. "I want to tell you something, Callie," he said. "If my father ever . . . if you ever hear from my father, stay away from him. Don't ever believe a word he says."

Still aghast, Callie stared at him. She

felt the tightness of dread in her chest. "Who was it you saw in the living room talking to Emery and Dorothy . . . that bothered you so much?"

He didn't answer.

"Just tell me one thing," she said, at last. "Did you see Emery and Dorothy anywhere again after you went down to the boathouse?"

He studied her hard for a moment, then he looked away. "Callie, you remember what that last hour was like. I don't remember who I saw. Or didn't see. All right?"

I remember who I didn't see, she thought. I looked everywhere.

She didn't know if he was lying or telling the truth, but she knew she couldn't push it any farther, for now. As if he had picked up on her danger signs and sensed her growing uncertainty, he reached out and brushed her cheek with the backs of his fingers. "You scare the hell out of me when you do that."

"Do what?" she muttered. She never got an answer.

He was looking out over the parking lot. "We've got company," he said.

Involuntarily, Callie straightened, her eyes following his gaze. "Where?"

"On the other side of the gas pumps. That's his Lincoln." Malcolm turned and looked at her. "It's him."

"Who? The reporter?" she said.

At first, nothing seemed to move. There was a stark quality about every detail of the scene—the wall of plate-glass windows facing the parking lot, the sunlight glancing off the roofs of cars, the service station fifty yards away. The whole thing sat frozen before her like a photograph.

"No doubt about it," he said. "You see it?"

"No, not yet."

Then she did. Her eyes narrowed on the far back corner of the service station. Yes, there it was—visible in the spaces between gas pumps—a steel-gray Lincoln. Callie reached across the table and took his hand. The way the Lincoln was parked made it impossible to tell who, if anyone, was inside it.

"This isn't funny," she said. "What do you think he wants?"

Malcolm didn't answer. The waitress came with their orders. Orange juice and a

Danish for Callie and Malcolm's sunrise special. The woman leaned across the table, stretching her saggy arms to deliver the plates and refill their coffee cups.

Malcolm waited until she was gone to push his plate away. "I'm not hungry after all," he said, still studying the parking lot. "Let's not stay here too long."

Callie sipped her coffee and put down the cup. "Okay," she said. With a gesture of impatience, Malcolm scooted his chair back and stood up. "Then let's go. I can't stand it here." He signaled the waitress and asked for the check. "We're in a hurry."

"Everybody's always in a hurry," the waitress said, tearing the ticket from her pad and dropping it by the ashtray.

He left a tip and picked up the bill as Callie rose beside him. She had promised herself that she would follow his lead, do what he asked her to do, without question. Together they made their exit between tables. "When we get outside," he said, "act as if we don't have a clue." On the wall behind the counter, a large clock showed 11:39. The cashier's eyes lingered a little too long on Callie while Malcolm paid, but they managed to get outside to the car without anyone asking for an autograph.

Callie walked at his side. At the gas station, the steel-gray Lincoln had not moved. Malcolm took a hasty reconnaissance of the entire area as they approached the Mercedes. And Callie did the same, but other than the Lincoln, nothing looked out of place to her. She hardly knew what to expect. Do what he says, she kept telling herself. It'll be all right.

Malcolm unlocked her door, let her in, closed the door and went around. A moment later, they were safe inside the car. "Put on your seat belt," he said, "good and tight." He started the engine, shifted into reverse, swung back and around, changed gears and they were moving forward at low speed.

Callie asked, "What are you going to do?" but his concentration was fixed on what lay before them.

Malcolm turned into the open lane dividing the rows of cars. The distance to the Lincoln closed slowly, then even more slowly until they had stopped altogether. The Lincoln's side windows were dark glass; she still couldn't see who was in it.

Barely thirty feet separated them now. "There's one thing he can't do," Malcolm told her as he readjusted the rearview mirror. "He can't keep up with us . . . he can't outrun us. Not in a rented Lincoln." Again he let his foot off the brake and they began to roll forward.

"Mal," Callie said, feeling more and more uncertain, "what are you doing?"

"This has to stop," he said and she saw his jaw muscles twitch. "I've had it."

"Please . . . let's just get out of here."

All at once, he hit the brakes, shifted into park and threw open his door. Callie reached for him, to stop him, but too late. Malcolm was already out of the car and bearing down on the Lincoln. She got out herself, but she had only gone a few steps before he had reached the rear of the Lincoln and was moving up along its steel-gray flank. "Mal, don't!" Callie's said but her plea hardly carried. It was all happening incredibly fast.

His fist clenched, Malcolm grabbed the handle and flung the door open. No one was there. At the same time, a older man rushed from the filling station—a tall, balding man in a red golf shirt. "Young man," he shouted, "what do you think you're doing?"

Malcolm snapped straight and turned.

Callie had never seen the man before—clearly Malcolm hadn't either. He stood riveted beside the open door.

"Why are you in my car?"

Embarrassed, Malcolm opened his hands out before him. "I'm sorry," he said, sheepishly. "I thought you were someone else. I apologize. I'm sorry." He started backing away. After a few steps he turned and came trotting back to the Mercedes. "Let's go, Callie," he said. "I feel like a fool."

He cranked the wheel hard; the Mercedes spun onto the highway. He started to laugh. And it was such a good, infectious laugh, so much the Malcolm she loved, that she began to laugh, too. They laughed and laughed together. "Did you see the look on his face?" he said, as if he had been caught in a prank. "No," she replied, feeling tremendous relief, "but I saw the look on yours."

He pushed his foot to the floor and the speedometer swung across the dial, the power of the Mercedes still not fully unleashed. "I'm sorry," he said. "What am I doing? I'm driving you crazy. I'm driving myself crazy. No more of this. Honey, we're free." He put his arm around her shoulders and drew her over. "Don't ever forget I love you," he said and his eyes held hers for a moment, all the promises still there.

Stop looking for trouble, Callie thought and moved closer. You're on your honeymoon.

"I never forget," she said.

Back in the parking lot, behind the wheel of a dusty Mercury station wagon, Harwood waited until they were gone from sight and the monitor's blue bead flashed faster and faster, before he pulled out after them.

The countryside began to slip past in a blinding green blur; the force of gravity thrust Callie back against her seat. The needle sank past 80, then 90 and kept on going. Top speed was 160. She wanted to tell him not to go for it, but when she tried to speak, the wind filled her throat so completely she couldn't utter a sound.

It was insane to move that fast on a two-lane blacktop, but Callie didn't—

couldn't—interfere. On the steering wheel, his hands were square and strong and capable. Hands that took care of things, a husband's hands. Hands that held her. When she looked again, the needle had edged past 120, closer to 125.

Built for speed, the Mercedes performed flawlessly. Not the slightest tremor, nothing on earth like the sound of the air screaming over its coal-black skin. Malcolm pushed it up past 130 and looked over at her. His lips were parted and she could see the white gleam of his teeth. The speed was exhilarating like infinitesimal bubbles singing through her veins and Callie tried to allow herself to surrender to it—but she couldn't.

He quickly backed it down to 80. Then on down to 60. As soon as he could safely rein it in, Malcolm wheeled the Mercedes over onto the shoulder and drew her over in his arms and kissed her. "We're in the clear, I think. No one knows where we are. No one." He started to laugh again. "Ahhh, God," he said, putting his arm around her, "that was funny. Knock on wood, but I think maybe we've done it."

. . . I think maybe we've done it . . . we've done it . . . Malcolm's words echoed soothingly in her mind. They—the two of them—had done it. The tension that had overshadowed them throughout the morning suddenly gave way to euphoria.

"We've got to make the most of this."

Yes, she thought, feeling an overpowering need to celebrate. They started up again. Only a few minutes had passed before they came to a narrow two-lane highway that veered south and, looking back one last time, Malcolm swerved onto it. The road rose and fell with the undulating farmland, smooth on the short straightaways, tight around curves—the sort of road the nimble suspension of the Mercedes was designed for. The hunted look was leaving Malcolm's eyes, his mood steadily improving. "No one would ever expect us to go this way," he said. They were still passing everything else on the road, but to Callie it was as though the earth had slowed in its rotation.

It was a beautiful afternoon, the sky clear blue, the glorious sun shining—one of those times in late summer when the hot weather had begun to lose its strength and the world became a more temperate and hospitable place. Driving with one hand, Malcolm put his arm around her, drew her over and kissed her gently and the atmosphere was utterly transformed.

After Visalia they followed highway 198 through the little sun-baked towns of the San Joaquin Valley: Hanford and Armona, Coalinga and Priest Valley. The gas gauge had fallen to empty by the time they caught sight of a sign for a gas station, not far from San Lucas. Callie hardly had time to feel relieved before Malcolm was signaling left and turning in.

While the tank was being filled and Malcolm drank a cold beer at the counter, Callie tried to telephone the Hudson's Lake Arrowhead number, just to check in. The walls of the booth were covered with graffiti —obscenities overlaid with hearts pierced by arrows. Miles away, the phone rang and rang but no one answered, and Callie finally hung up.

"Who were you calling?" Malcolm asked as she approached.

"I wanted to leave word for Dorothy

and Emery in case they phone in. But no luck."

"When were they supposed to get back?"

"I don't remember," she said. "A week, I think."

"So," he said, "there you are."

On a state map, the attendant sketched a route for them with his finger while Malcolm leaned forward, studying it along with him. Look how interested he is, Callie thought with a smile. He was hopelessly, reassuringly normal. The rage she'd glimpsed in him last night and again just a while ago had been a momentary thing. Nothing else. This was where she needed to focus her attention. On the here and now. And now they were free.

But she still couldn't stop thinking about Emery's note.

"It's the long way around," the attendant was saying, "but it'll get you there."

"Thanks," Malcolm said.

As they returned to the car, she was aware that they didn't even hold hands. It was as if there was no need of that now— their possession of each other was so total.

A little thing; and yet, she missed it. Back on the road, they avoided the heavily traveled Highway 101 and took Route 22 instead, south and west toward Big Sur.

"I've never told you this," he said, "but I remember seeing you once the summe before we started college. You were down at the lake in a white bathing suit you used to have and I was standing there on the sand watching you. God, you were something to see."

Callie realized he must not have shaved that morning; she ran her fingers over his lovely dark bristle. She told him she still owned that white bathing suit but she never wore it anymore and he said, "I want you to put it on," and she said, "No, are you kidding?" and he said, "Come on. I swear I've never seen anything so beautiful in my life. I really wish you would." All right, maybe, Callie told him, when they got back. "If I can still get it on," she said.

That afternoon, it seemed as if they were able to stop the clock and live completely in the sun. Only now was she beginning to think of herself as Callie Rhodes, after living all her life as Callie McKenna.

The past did not exist, the future did not exist. She said to him, "In one hour, forty-two and a half minutes, we will have been married for two days. Does that seem possible to you?" He looked at her with his best grin.

Through that long afternoon Callie felt as though they were gliding through life, hardly touching the ground. The lunch they had on the sun porch in Monterey, the slow, meandering walk through the maze of galleries and antique shops; the quiet talk they had about the future, Malcolm doing most of the talking, the life they would have together. Two souls in perfect concert. Two lives lived as one. The drive into San Francisco, cocktails at sunset, nibbling German pretzels and the wonderful flowing sense of intimacy; sometimes without a word they laughed at exactly the same moment because they were thinking exactly the same thing; sometimes he kissed her up the elevator, sometimes they waited until they were behind the door, Malcolm, his head resting on her bare stomach, gazing up at her while she stroked his hair; the moment at dinner, when sitting beside her at the table, he discovered that underneath the black skirt she was wearing nothing at all and then later, her lips against his golden cheek when even his aftershave was like some wild elixir.

Day Four—Morning
San Francisco

8

In the florist shop of the Vandeveer Hotel, a lovely smiling girl came toward him and said, "Could I help you, sir? Those roses are fresh today. Aren't they extraordinary?"

The long-stemmed red roses stood in a ten-gallon bucket at his fingertips, but Harwood moved on. "Yes," he said, "but, I don't think . . . not roses."

She turned her head, her smile slipping away, surprised at the hardness in his voice.

He continued to examine the profusion of flowers. Finally his hand went out and lightly touched a delicate, waxy petal the color of an opal. "Maybe one of these," he said thoughtfully. There were only two of the orchids in the narrow Chinese vase of hammered bronze.

"They were flown in this morning from Guatemala," the girl said. With care, she removed one of the stems from the other. He saw how much she admired it as she held it in the cup of her hand.

"Perfect," he said.

"Would you like it in a corsage?"

Harwood considered for a moment. "That would seem a shame. Couldn't we just arrange it in a small vase? Something quite simple?"

"Of course."

The girl was a few minutes putting it together. Standing in the cool fragrant shop, watching faces go by the window, aware all the time of the girl's quick, delicate fingers, he felt the anxiety wash over him. One false step and Malcolm—

"Is this what you had in mind?"

She had done it well. Held in place by small, clear marbles, the orchid and sprig of spider fern stood in a thin vase of etched glass.

"Yes, exactly. Would it be possible to have this delivered? You see, my son and his wife are here on their honeymoon and I'd like to give them . . . some token."

"Oh, that's sweet," the girl said.

"I was thinking . . . if they ordered from room service, could this be sent along with their tray?" He slid the orchid back across the counter toward her. "You see, I don't want them to know I was here. It would have to be our secret."

"Of course, I understand." She took it from him. "Let me see what I can do." She asked for their names and he gave her both their names, explaining that he didn't know how they were registered or which room they were in, perhaps the bridal suite.

"Then . . . perhaps you would like a card," she said, indicating the display of tiny, discreet cards and removing the bag from the orchid.

"No card. I want it to be a surprise. And I'd like the other orchid arranged just like this one. For you."

The girl seemed not to understand or perhaps she thought she had heard him incorrectly. He saw a faint blush heat her cheeks. "Really, I couldn't . . ."

Harwood removed a few bills from his wallet. "Don't disappoint me. How much, altogether?"

"You mean—for two?"

He nodded.

"Well . . . they're awfully expensive.

They're thirty dollars each. I'd really rather—''

"No, please," he interrupted, "I'd like you to have it." Again he opened his wallet, taking out an additional fifty-dollar bill. "Please, ring it up. How much does it come to, with tax?"

The girl told him, then reluctantly took the money and gave him change.

He leaned across the miniature Japanese garden, like a doll's garden, and lifted the second orchid from the bronze vase, passing it to her. She smiled again suddenly. "Thank you. It's very nice of you."

Harwood thanked her again and walked out into the lobby, looking at his watch. Almost two in the afternoon.

On the mezzanine a few minutes later, he found a place with a view down the hall to the kitchen and sat in a club chair to wait. Ten minutes passed. Twenty minutes. Only two carts draped in white were wheeled from the kitchen, down the hall and into a side elevator, each bearing a small bouquet of summer flowers, zinnias and daylilies.

Below the elaborate iron railing, the crowd in the lobby had gradually dispersed. It occurred to him that perhaps the bride and groom wouldn't order from room service. The fact that it had been after midnight when they arrived increased the chances they were still upstairs, but maybe they had somehow gotten by him unseen and gone out for lunch. Or it was possible they had even left earlier. In the end, he had to trust the florist to find a way to deliver the orchid.

A half hour went by, then forty-five minutes, and again the kitchen doors swung open and a waiter emerged pushing a cart—a cart draped in white and bearing his orchid in a thin glass vase. *There it is.*

When the waiter pushed the tray into the elevator, he was joined by a tall man dressed in a business suit and carrying a briefcase.

"How pretty," Callie said, leaning toward the opal-colored orchid and breathing its delicate scent. "You had them do this, didn't you? You're such a sweet old grumpy bear."

"No, not me. It must have been one of your other admirers."

It had been raining all day long, a quiet summer rain, and they had slept in, blissfully, under the constant patter of drops striking the windows. Settling the breakfast tray between them, Malcolm sat on the side of the bed and began to feed Callie orange juice and toast. With his free hand he smoothed away the tendrils of red-gold hair that were curling around her face. He kissed her lightly on the ear. "I'm not sweet, I'm not old and I'm not grumpy. I am, however, a bear."

"Yes, you are," she said, "and handsome as can be, too. What's this?"

A square, white envelope stood between the salt shaker and the sugar bowl. She tore open the letterhead stationery and held it up for both of them to read. The note was handwritten on the heavy vellum of the hotel; the management extended congratulations on their wedding and, as a courtesy of the hotel, offered them complimentary tickets to the Black and White Ball.

"So that explains it," Callie said. "The hotel must've sent the orchid. What an nice touch."

The tickets were for that evening at eight, dress was formal, masks optional. Callie was delighted, and Malcolm was equally enthusiastic. "I've heard of the

Black and White, haven't you? I've heard it's incredible."

"I'm going to twirl you around," he said, "like you've never been twirled before. This will be my first chance to show you off."

She immediately got on the telephone with their acceptance. They made dinner reservations for six and then Callie talked to the concierge, requesting her to come to their suite to help attend to the details.

"I didn't bring a dinner jacket," Malcolm said. "If we're going to do this, I've got things I have to do."

"You gotta do what you gotta do." Callie disentangled herself and walked naked into the bathroom to fetch a robe. While he showered and shaved and quickly dressed, she finished her coffee.

When he was ready, Callie followed him to the door between rooms and kissed him good-bye. "Ummm," she said, "you smell good," running her hand up under his polo shirt and across his firm, flat stomach, but Malcolm backed away from her hand and laughed. "Okay, I'm going," he said. A moment later, she heard him shut the door on his way out.

It was a rainy, miserable afternoon, all the more miserable for it being August. Despite the air conditioning, a clinging dampness had penetrated the rooms, making her feel uncomfortable and clammy. Even with the bedroom lights turned on, it was still dreary. Callie looked at her watch; it was going on 3:45 already. A lot to do, she thought, and not much time to do it in. She opened the closet, debating what she would wear, when she heard a knock at the door.

Only a couple of minutes had passed since Malcolm had left and she ran to get it. "Now what have you forgotten?" she said, as she opened the door.

But it wasn't Malcolm.

A man was standing there at the doorway, a tall, shadowy man. It caught her completely off guard. Her heart beat violently. She tried to say, "Yes," but she was actually incapable of speaking.

His outline was dim in the meager daylight of the hall. "You must be Callie," he said.

Callie? The fact that he called her by her first name made her even more wary. "Yes, I'm Callie," she got out at last.

"I'm sorry if I frightened you." The man extended his hand. "Preston Harwood. Please don't be afraid. I'm Malcolm's father."

Uncontrollably her heart gave a leap of apprehension; for a moment she was too surprised to move or even to speak. Now that she could see him more clearly, it was unnerving how much he looked like Malcolm, she realized. He was older, of course, his hair going to silver, but the family resemblance was striking. The eyes, she thought. I should have known those eyes; I thought I'd know them anywhere.

And yet, when she shook his hand, she was immediately aware how hard and damp his fingers were. "Malcolm's father?"

"Yes," he said, "could I come in?" but as he spoke, down the hall the whir of the rising elevator drained his attention. His head turned toward the elevator doors and, for a moment, he seemed deadly afraid—Callie could feel the fear radiate from him like an aura.

Without waiting for an invitation, he stepped inside the door and, even with Callie clutching the doorknob, he pushed the door shut behind them.

"Malcolm's not here," she tried to explain. "You've just missed him."

"Yes, I know. Look, I've got to speak to you. Can I please come in? It's urgent."

He walked past her, through the foyer and into the living room. It was only then she realized she was still clasping the doorknob in a death grip.

Recovering from her surprise, Callie followed him in silence. He was carrying a briefcase, which he put down on the carpet. Having Malcolm's father here, in her bridal suite, was the last thing she had ever expected and yet, he walked ahead of her toward the gray light of the rainy windows as if he knew exactly what he was doing. It was definitely his eyes that were most like Malcolm, she decided now. His eyes and his voice and the way he moved.

Two sofas flanked the fireplace and Callie took up a place behind one of them near a huge bouquet of day-old flowers. Only half aware that she was establishing a barrier between them, Callie continued to study him for a couple of seconds. *Malcolm said to stay away from him.*
What does he want?

Harwood spoke first. "I'm sorry to appear out of the blue like this . . . but there didn't seem to be another way."

"How did you ever . . . ?"

Suddenly there were footsteps outside the door, someone running. His head twisted toward the sound and he stood braced facing the door until the sound passed away. He let out a breath and visibly collected himself. When he spoke again, his voice was hard, rushed. "When will he be back?"

"I'm not sure. Soon," she lied. "I expect him any time."

The door to the bedroom stood open a few inches and she saw that he was looking through it at the small round table draped in linen, which held the remnants of their breakfast and the orchid in the glass vase. Listen, Callie," he said, turning back to her, "we only have a few minutes. You have to listen to me. There are things—important things—you've got to know."

Callie felt she was being drawn into the middle of something against her will. "If it's really important, I'd rather you talked to Malcolm about it."

He glanced at his watch surreptitiously, and then looked around at the door, all while he was saying, "I'm afraid you don't understand. That's why I came to see you. I don't think you know what you've done— what you've gotten yourself into."

Suddenly she felt her heart beating where her abdomen pressed against the sofa—she realized she was straining against it with all her strength. And growing more and more frightened.

"Excuse me," she said, unsteadily, "but you're making me really uncomfortable. I haven't done anything."

"Don't you see, I had to come here." He wiped his forehead with a handkerchief. "I don't know where to start. I know you're under the impression that his name is Rhodes. But it's not. His name's Harwood, like mine."

"*Harwood? My* Malcolm? I don't get it. What're you saying—that Malcolm lied to me?" Callie stood rock still, conscious of her stance, conscious even of the hang of her robe.

He moved closer to her. "Where is Malcolm?"

"What are you trying to tell me?" she asked again and the thought flew through her mind: My God, who have I married?

"What's he been telling you?" Harwood said. "Has he told you about me?" He took a step toward her. "What did he say? You think you know him, Callie . . . but you don't."

Never taking her eyes from him for a moment, she couldn't comprehend at all what he wanted, what he expected of her. "I don't believe you," she said. "Why are you telling me these things? I don't believe a word you say."

All at once it struck her. This was the man she had seen two days ago—standing below her balcony. The man who had frightened her so badly, whom she had taken for a reporter.

"Listen, Callie. You have to be very careful about Malcolm. Don't make him angry. And another thing . . ."

"No," she interrupted him. "No!" Callie realized suddenly that all the time he was speaking, he was also edging toward her. She tried to counteract this by moving slightly farther away from him, pressing herself against the side of the table and wondering if she could slip past and make for the door. She took a couple of tentative steps but he reached out and swiftly held her by the shoulder. She felt the press of his fingers dig into her so strongly she could hardly move.

He was saying, "You may not know it yet, but Malcolm is sick. When he begins to lose control, he thinks everyone's against him."

"Let go!" She twisted from him and backed away. "How dare you come in here and say that. Malcolm warned me about you."

"That's right! There's no telling what he's told you about me—what lies he's told you."

"I want you to go," she said, feeling her own voice tightening down. "I won't be involved in anything like this. I've got to talk to Malcolm."

"No, Callie." Harwood's entire expression, even the muscles in his face, seemed to grow harder and more defined. "Don't let him know I've been to see you. It's really important that you don't talk to anyone about this, Callie, to anyone . . . because then Malcolm will find out."

"Get out of here right now! I mean it! Malcolm told me never to believe you."

Quickly he picked up his briefcase and

opened it. "Don't believe me! What about this?" From inside the briefcase, he took out a thick manila folder overstuffed with papers, which he left lying on the cushioned seat of the sofa. "Look this over! This is what we have to live with. I'm only trying to protect you . . . *You don't believe me!* These are not lies. Remember—Callie— above all, don't get him angry."

He closed the briefcase and grabbed it up. "He must not see this file—he must not know you have it. Whatever you do, be careful. I'll be around. I'm going to try to follow—in case you . . ."

"I don't want you to leave that thing," Callie said.

"There're things you have to know. I have no choice."

"I won't look at it, I promise you. Take it with you . . ."

"Callie, you've got to trust me! *Trust me!* I can't do any more than this. Not until he . . . not until something happens." He vanished into the foyer. After a moment, the door shut.

Her ears were ringing and her legs wouldn't stop trembling.

She couldn't believe it. How dare he

say those things to her. Monstrous. Her head was still spinning and she realized she had covered her ears. She felt as though her life were seeping away through every pore in her body.

The file sat there on the white damask of the sofa like a coiled and deadly snake. It was about an inch thick, tied around and across with twine and also held together by two thick rubber bands. The spine of the folder itself had been reinforced with strapping tape and the outside cover was badly soiled and coffee-stained, its edges torn and frayed. Lifting a lock of hair from her face, Callie leaned over, examining it. The typewritten label affixed to it was dingy, badly worn. It stated simply: THE STATE OF MICHIGAN V. MALCOLM PRESTON HARWOOD.

The words themselves sent a chill down her spine. They sounded so official— so legal and absolute. What could it be? she wondered. *Malcolm, what did you do?* From the ragged appearance of the folder, it must have happened a long time ago.

How wooden and cold her hands were; they hung from her body like the hands of a doll. All at once she began to tremble all over. There was a bitter taste in her throat:

she felt dizzy and sick. The sun had come out, but now the suite, brimming with sunlight, suddenly seemed more desolate than ever before, a stillness running through it like water, filling its depths.

Now that she had noticed the label, her impulse was to tear it open and see what it contained. Maybe I should, Callie thought, at the same time weighing how furious Malcolm would be when she told him how the file came to be here. A voice in her head kept reminding her that some things are better left undisturbed. Only fear held her back, fear like a force of gravity. Let sleeping dogs lie, she thought. She wished there was some way she could return it unopened to Malcolm's father—but she didn't know how. "Throw it at him," she said aloud to herself. "I'd throw it at him—throw it right back in his face."

God help me. What an awful thing for anyone to do. Anyone—least of all a father. Despite his father's warnings, she wished Malcolm were there. And yet . . . no, what am I thinking? She went to the door, locked and chained it, walked back into the living room and stood there, rudderless, surrounded by the large windows that overlooked the city. She went directly to the telephone and pushed zero for the concierge. "Yes, Mrs. Rhodes," the woman answered, "how may I help you?"

Callie explained that she needed to get in touch with her husband. Was it possible that he had inquired about a place to get a dinner jacket? The woman said he had not; Callie thanked her, put the receiver down and tried, forcibly, to relax. She had no idea what she was going to say to him, only that she had to tell him what had happened; she would tell him everything. She wasn't about to start her marriage by keeping things from him. And yet, his father's warning stuck fast in her brain like a fishhook: *Don't get him angry.*

No matter how much Callie tried to avoid it, her eyes kept straying to the old manila folder stuffed with papers.

The glorious late afternoon sun was shining. She stood there, looking at her watch and waiting—waiting for Malcolm to come back. It was going on 5:15. Their dinner reservations were for 6:00. He's probably on his way right now, she thought. She felt weak. Helpless. I don't want to know anything about this, she thought.

She began to walk around nervously, picking things up and putting them down, without it ever once registering what they were. Finally she couldn't stand it any longer. She had to get rid of the file, and to hell with the consequences. She wished to God Malcolm's father had never brought it. What if Malcolm had been in trouble years ago? No one could go back and change it now. All she could think to do was to dispose of the damned thing. Get rid of it! she thought. Get rid of it!

Taking the file with her, Callie ran to the bedroom and threw on shorts and a T-shirt. Already her resolve was waning. She felt an overwhelming urge to tear the file open and see what was in it. But she knew better. It was dangerous; it would be like running her fingers along a cold, sharp blade, daring it to cut her.

With the file clutched in her arm, she went to the door, opened it and stepped out into the hall. All around her, the hotel was silent. At the end of the carpeted hall and around the corner, she passed through metal service doors and entered a vestibule that housed the ice maker and a Coke machine. A few steps farther and she came to narrow door marked housekeeping.

Callie slowly rotated on her toes, looking around to make sure she wasn't seen. No one else was watching her. The knob turned in her hand; the door swung open on a broom closet, the shelves lined with cleaning supplies. In an instant, she was inside.

It was hard to focus in the dimness. A large garbage can, filled nearly to the top with paper and trash, sat only a few feet away. Gingerly, she lifted the layer of newspapers and slid the thick file down along the inside of the plastic bag until it was entirely lost from sight. As if a tremendous weight had been lifted, relief spread through her. But she had no time to lose; she ran back to the suite.

Still the thought of the file hung over the whirl of her preparations for the evening. The concierge arrived, dispensed advice and took Callie's evening gown to be pressed. Even a long hot bath, usually so soothing, did nothing to alleviate her fearful curiosity.

By 5:35, she was about ready. Her

gown and a matching mask of blue-black feathers arrived as promised, right on time. She opened her makeup case and for the next five minutes or so, she put the finishing touches on her makeup. The evening gown slid down over her arms and enfolded her.

A room away, she heard Malcolm coming in the front door. For a moment longer, she continued to gaze at her troubled eyes until she could make her expression more reliable. "I'm in here," she called.

Dressed formally for the evening in a white dinner jacket, carrying his street clothes on a hanger, Malcolm came through the bedroom door on his way to the closet. "You look sensational," he said.

It was an act of will for Callie to put on a smooth, innocent expression as she faced him. "Thanks," she said with a smile, "you look pretty ravishing yourself." She concentrated on putting on an earring. For all she wanted to tell him, she could find nothing to say, except, "It seems like ages, doesn't it . . . since we saw each other?"

"Ages," he concurred, as he hung up his clothes.

He walked toward her, close, closer.

His jacket still smelled faintly of cleaning fluid. Leaning over, he kissed the tip of her nose. "I love to look at your eyes. You have the most beautiful eyes."

Callie turned her face away from him for a moment, moved by the feeling his tenderness produced in her. And yet, a tiny doubt smoldered within her, dampened down but ready to burst into flame that would devour her completely.

"What have you been doing all afternoon?" he said casually, hardly glancing up.

"Oh, you know," she said, "sometimes things take longer—and this was on such a spur of the moment . . ." Irritated with herself for being so unprepared and lying so badly, she felt compelled to elaborate. But she knew the more she said, the worse it would get. Even though she was an actress, and a good one, she was not an accomplished liar.

"What's the matter then?" Malcolm said. "You seem tense—"

She could feel the little web of lies and omissions already beginning to entrap her. With her face still averted, Callie changed the subject. "I'm starved. Shouldn't we go down to dinner now?"

Malcolm grinned at her evasion and checked his watch. "Yes," he said, "it's time."

9

A sense of celebration pervaded the hotel dining room that evening and it was lucky for her, Callie thought. Her nervousness, the fact that her hands were damp and she clenched up at the slightest thing, could all be explained away by the air of excitement swirling around them. When they sat down, she realized she actually was ravenous and, at the same time, she felt almost sick with uncertainty. Maybe it was a mistake, she thought, to throw that file away. Each time Malcolm looked up, she quickly turned away to keep him from seeing the questions in her eyes. And the feeling of time passing began to weigh on her endlessly.

She attempted to divert his attention and talk to him. "You know, Malcolm," she said, "you haven't told me much about what it was like when you were growing up."

He only looked at her and smiled. "I don't want to talk about it, Callie," he said gently. "That's all ancient history."

She took a sip of her ice water. "But I want to know everything about you. What could be so awful?"

His grin was a slightly lopsided. He just shrugged. "I'm in a great mood tonight," he said, finally, "and nothing's going to change it."

She talked and talked, continuously fanning the little coals of her subtle interrogation. She was desperate for him to tell her what she yearned to know—that there was nothing to fear. But it was no use. The more she tried, the less she succeeded. Until finally she fell silent.

Malcolm was quiet, too. They were both aware of the festive hubbub in the room, the constant movement of glamorous people around them, the light clatter of plates and silverware, voices on the air, titillating laughter. Still, Callie's thoughts kept returning inexorably to the afternoon and the unnerving presence of Malcolm's father. *And the file.* The entire fabric of the evening had been altered by that damned file. Before long, she found herself wondering if the custodians had already taken away the trash upstairs—while the hands of the clock above the arched doorway marked the passage of time in slow, grinding steps.

No matter what she did, she couldn't get away from it: the image of the file kept plowing through her brain.

They were finishing dessert when a man's voice said, "Callie? Callie McKenna?"

They turned. Angling toward them was a man she recognized as Phil Demerest, who was in turn trailing an attractive redhead behind him. He had been a fledgling screenwriter when she met him on the set of *Afterlife,* and now he was a very successful independent producer. Farther back, looking sleek and unruffled, came another couple that Callie only vaguely recognized, although she had seen them before in the company of Phil Demerest.

"Who's this?" Malcolm asked her under his breath.

"Old acquaintances," she muttered, and then turning to the two couples as Malcolm stood, she said, "I'm not Callie

McKenna anymore. I'd like you to meet my husband, Malcolm Rhodes.''

The men shook hands. ''You're married! My God!'' Phil said, breaking into a mischievous, disarming smile. ''This is Brigitte Brocca, who warms my heart.'' The redhead looked shy under the sudden attention and Callie liked her immediately. ''And I think you know Jack and Linda Schultz.''

''Yes, I believe so,'' Callie replied and everyone said hello and began talking at once.

It had been months since they had seen each other, and the first few minutes passed in pleasantries. Only Brigitte hung back; she was tall and lithesome and tanned, and a little windblown from a day at the beach. She was wearing dark blue velvet that caught the sparkle of her eyes.

''Are you two here with anyone?'' Demerest said. ''Could you join us?''

Callie glanced around at Malcolm, as if entreating him to tell her what to do, but by then it was too late. ''Well, then,'' Phil Demerest said, ''it's settled. You've got to come join us at our table. We've got ringside seats and plenty of room. If you haven't been to one of these orgies, you owe it to yourself."

"Oh, Phil, I don't know. Darling, what do you think?"

"Yes," Malcolm said. "We'd be delighted."

After he had signed for their bill and Callie and the other two women had settled into their feather masks, the six of them made their way out of the dining room, across the hall and through the crowd at the entrance to the ballroom. A look of utter trust and vulnerability came over Brigitte's face when she and Callie were side by side for a moment. "I'm a big fan," she admitted in an appealing, girlish way. "I loved you in *Afterlife.* I cried and cried."

It was good to hear flattering words again. "It's nice of you to say so," Callie told her. "I was lucky to get that part."

The ballroom was crowded all the way through the adjoining bar and spilled out through windows and doors onto the terraces as if the place had burst its seams. Phil Demerest's table was on the south terrace with a good view through one of the huge Palladian windows to the stage and the dance floor. Behind them, the other outdoor tables, six or eight deep, were taken, and people stood between them, drinking and talking.

Waiters and waitresses danced to the bar, then danced back again, trays balanced high above their heads laden with drinks. By 9:45, some of the guests were dancing in long conga lines—it seemed the only way to get from one place to another.

Champagne was served and served freely and the conversation spiraled around them. Callie, though, had the panicky feeling that things were slipping more and more out of control and she didn't know what to do about it. She wished suddenly that she could be back upstairs, alone, with that file safely back in her possession. She didn't belong here at all. Not tonight. And she couldn't just sit here and do nothing.

She waited until shortly after ten before she leaned to Malcolm and said, "Excuse me, darling. I need to freshen up. I'll be right back."

But when she stood to leave, Brigitte Brocca got up, too. "Oh," she whispered delightedly, "if you're going to the powder room, I'll go with you."

Callie could think of no way to uninvite

her. They wormed their way through the crowd and out into the lobby, toward the ladies room across the hall. Women were waiting in a line that curved through the door. Suddenly, Callie started to back away. "I'll see you back at the table, Brigitte. I've got to get a breath of air."

"Me, too. I'll come along."

"No. Please. I don't mean to be rude, but I need to make a couple of quick phone calls. And I've got to rustle up a couple of aspirin. I'll see you back at the table." Callie turned and walked into the crowd.

With a look over her shoulder to make certain she wasn't followed, she took the ornate staircase to the crowded mezzanine and made her way to the bank of elevators. Only two other people were waiting: a middle-aged businessman, who was leafing through the evening newspaper, and a woman, probably his wife, carrying a shopping bag from Ghirardelli Square. When the sliding doors opened, a gaggle of teenage girls in pink formals swarmed out. The man folded his paper and held the elevator door first for the woman with the bag and then for Callie, and got on himself. He pushed 7.

The woman pushed 9—so they weren't together, after all—and Callie pushed 10.

They rode up in silence.

Even with Brigitte returning to the table alone, Callie figured she had ten minutes—and maybe as much as fifteen minutes—before Malcolm would begin to seriously wonder what had happened and come looking for her. She checked her watch. It was 10:22. To be on the safe side, she knew she had to be back downstairs and headed toward the table no later than 10:37. She folded her hands behind her, feeling the seconds ticking off in her brain.

The man got off on 7. For several seconds the door remained open. Impatiently Callie hit the CLOSE DOOR button, but to no avail. Too late, she wished she had waited for an empty elevator and gone up alone—this was eating up too much time. Finally, with a slow wheeze, the doors slid shut.

The woman carrying the Ghirardelli shopping bag got off on 9. Across the landing, Callie noted that the metal service doors were propped open and custodians were pushing large blue garbage cans on wheels. Picking up the trash, she knew at once. If the men were working their way down from the tenth floor, Callie knew the file was now lost irretrievably. If they were working their way up from the basement, she still had a few minutes to get it back. But only a few.

She stepped off the elevator on 10 and automatically checked the time. 10:24. All that waiting had cost her two minutes. As she turned on her high heels, she heard a girl's giggles coming at her from down one of the halls. Then someone else—a boy, she thought—was laughing. That's the last thing Callie wanted—to be recognized and delayed by unruly fans.

Abruptly, she darted through the metal service doors and stepped backward past the Coke machine and the ice maker. But the rowdy voices, as if following her, grew even louder and closer than she'd expected.

It was impossible. She didn't want to be cornered here in the service area—in her evening gown. It would do wonders for her image, for word to get around that she had been in the Huntington Hotel going through the trash. Get in the storage room, she thought.

She went directly to the door marked

HOUSEKEEPING, drew it open and came to a complete stop. Now three identical trash cans were crammed into the small space. What was she going to do? There was not even room enough for her to get in and close the door without running the risk of dirtying her clothes. Wildly she cast about for a place where she could hide. The service stairs loomed behind her, shadowed and dark. A moment later, as the laughter and the voices burst through the metal doors, Callie vanished under the stairs.

Three fraternity boys and a girl ambled in, laughing and stumbling against each other, half-drunk. "I told you, you'd be sorry," the girl giggled. "I told you, we'd get caught." The boys were attempting to buy Cokes from the machine, but the quarters spilled from their fingers and they had to go chasing after them across the concrete floor. They found this hilarious. Bending over with laughter, the girl scooped ice into a chrome bucket, the cubes bouncing and skittering at her feet when she dropped them.

Callie was conscious, intensely conscious, of time passing. It was 10:29. Then 10:30. Seven minutes remained. She tried to imagine what was happening downstairs. Certainly by now Brigitte would have re- turned to the table; Malcolm would be won- dering where she was and what had hap- pened to detain her. He might even be looking for her.

I've got to know what he did, Callie thought. I can't help it. I have to know.

The boys, their arms laden with cans of Coke, and the girl, carrying her ice bucket, walked out. 10:33. Four minutes to go and that was pushing it. Callie couldn't wait any longer.

As if materializing from the gloom of the stairs, Callie ran to the storage room. It had occurred to her that if the maids had placed two additional containers in the room, then the one farthest back should be the original trash can where she had stuck the file. At least it seemed the best chance she had. She set her beaded evening bag aside on one of the shelves. All of a sudden, only a few feet away, she heard the whine of the service elevator. Across from the ice machine, the noise magnified and stopped with a hard clang.

Callie fought her way past the first two trash cans, to the third in back, and dug down under the stacks of newspapers, tossing them out around her when they got in her way. She could hear the elevator moving up and down with hard metallic jolts as the men leveled it with the floor. At last, her hands closed on the thick file and she drew it out. Yes, that was it. Callie glanced at the label bearing Malcolm's name and flushed with relief.

Seconds later, when the rasping doors parted and the two men came out of the elevator dragging large blue garbage cans on wheels, they saw a streak of black dress vanish through the service doors and the floor outside the storage room littered with a whirlwind of papers.

Callie ran to the suite and let herself in. 10:38. No time left! she thought. He's looking for me right now! She passed through the living room, shadows flickering around her, and into the bedroom where she slowly spun on her toes, searching for a place to hide the file. She stepped out of her heels and dropped her beaded bag on the vanity bench. Nowhere seemed secure.

All at once she stood straight and still. She could have sworn she heard the soft click of the door closing in the other room.

It's him! she thought. He's here! He's coming! If he found her in possession of the file now, how would she ever explain it?

Callie darted to the side of the bed, but she couldn't hide a clump of papers under the mattress—too risky; she twisted toward the dresser where she had put her underwear—still too chancy and obvious. She couldn't think. For a bare instant, she stood motionless. Then she heard a different sound—she was certain of it now—muffled footsteps on the carpet, soft as whispers, and then, a voice she knew so well.

"Callie?"

Malcolm's voice.

Grasping the battered file, she dashed to the master bath, closed the door to the width of her fingers and hastily flushed the toilet. Now where? *Where?*

One second.

Two seconds.

Every moment that passed drove her a little nearer to hysteria. Three seconds. Finally it occurred to her that the most obvious hiding place was probably the best—her eyes fastened on the two cabinet doors below the sink and she immediately pulled them open. Four seconds. There was no reason why Malcolm would go rummaging through this cabinet. She slid the manila file in behind a package of six rolls of toilet tissue, silently closed the doors and stood up.

Five seconds.

The door swung inward and Callie, drying her hands on a clean white towel, ran right into him. "God!" she gasped. "Malcolm! You startled me."

There was little doubt that he had been searching for her, and he met her now with a questioning look. She felt shaky and light-headed. His stare was leveled so squarely that she wanted to look behind her to see if she had made some glaring error. And knew she couldn't. Had she inadvertently let something slip? What did he already know?

"Are you all right?" he asked.

Unaware of what she was doing, Callie dropped the white towel and adjusted the top of her evening gown as though she needed to protect herself from him. "I'm fine," she said. "The lines were impossible downstairs and I decided to get away from

Brigitte for a few minutes. Have you been here long?"

"No, not long," he said. He grinned. "We were lost without you."

She put her arms around him. He laughed and tried to shrug off her embrace, but she clung to him, prolonging the moment.

"Better go," he said.

Callie felt herself wound tight with apprehension. I can't let on, she reminded herself. "Ohhh, do we have to?" she moaned with mock petulance, thinking, the sooner we get to bed, the sooner I can see that file. "Let's not go anywhere. Can't we just stay here?"

"What? And have all that wailing and gnashing of teeth? I think not."

"Surely we could think of something entertaining to do." She ran her hand under his jacket and up across his hard chest.

He laughed. "Come on, Callie. Cut it out."

"So conscientious," she said, teasingly. "I adore conscientious men." She could see he wasn't about to change his mind. "All right, lead the way."

He kissed her lightly and they turned

one after the other toward the door. If he had taken her hands or picked up the discarded towel, Malcolm might have realized that neither of them was even slightly wet.

10

She did not know how much later it was before the orchestra began to play Auld Lang Syne. When she discarded her mask and looked at her watch, it was a little past two in the morning. "Are we going?" she asked, her cheek resting on his lapel.

"Yes," Malcolm answered. "It's past your bedtime."

At a few of the other tables, the revelers continued their parties but the evening was breaking up. Glasses were speedily emptied and filled again with the last of the champagne as the stage lights went down. Then the house lights began to come on and Phil and Brigitte stood at their places, bidding everyone good-night, shaking hands, kissing cheeks, and little by little, the sound of muted laughter fluttered away like bright confetti.

Callie was suddenly, unexplainably, in

no hurry to go. The main entrance was crowded with people who were leaving, so she and Malcolm meandered back along the darker reaches of the terrace toward the front of the hotel. A little group of waiters and waitresses, who had been whispering confidences and comparing tips, were suddenly quiet. All eyes turned as she went by.

The glittering windows high above duplicated themselves in the many fountains and a gentle, melancholy breeze rippled over the chemical blue surface of the pool. Her mind, still a little fogged by the champagne, was clearing and all at once she became aware of something tugging painfully at her heart, an oppressive feeling of regret for having doubted him, neglected him. He should know what his father had done, she thought. Tell him. Tell him everything. As she turned to him, she rose on her toes, bringing up the mingled scent of her clothes and perfume, and for a moment her lips touched his. "Malcolm, wait a minute," she said. But she couldn't do it. She held on to his arm, breathing the night air that was now filled with mist, watching the blurred ribbons of taillights snake through the streets below. "I love you," she said, finally.

"I love you with all my heart. You know that, don't you?"

"That must be why you married me?" he said with a grin.

But her smile was fragile, ready to be broken and for an instant she felt totally unguarded and filled with compassion. "It's only you and me now. That's what you said. No one can harm us—not when we feel the way we do. Malcolm, let's go. We don't even have to go back to the room. The hotel could send us our things. Let's just get in the car and go—go to the airport and fly somewhere. Or we could go back home— no one would think to look for us at Emery's and they're away. Dorothy even suggested that we stay there. Why don't we run away together, really run away—right now? Right this minute. Please, Malcolm . . . wouldn't that be the best thing?"

He looked at her as if trying to fathom what was behind her words. He had been listening attentively and yet something about him changed, something about his eyes. "Back?" he asked.

"Yes."

"You mean back to L.A.? To the Hudsons'?"

"Yes," she said delightedly, "wouldn't it be a stroke of genius? Who would ever think to look for us . . ."

"You're kidding," he cut in. "Of course, we can't go back there."

Throat dry, she said, "Why can't we?"

"Because . . ." he replied. "Because we just can't." He continued to look at her for several seconds and when he couldn't any longer, he started to move away from her. "I'll see if we have any messages." She knew it was his way of dodging the question. No one would be leaving them messages.

There was so much more that she wanted to say and so much she wanted him to say, but Callie watched him go toward the lobby. Don't push it, she thought. Be careful.

In the distance behind her, the orchestra was disassembling instruments, folding cases. The last guests had gone. Callie trailed slowly and alone past the empty dining room where, earlier, a hundred fifty people had crowded among the lavish gold-leaf chairs. What am I going to do? she thought. I'll have to wait until he goes to sleep . . .

Her fears, for all her attempts at harnessing them, kept going round in a horrible maze of questions and clues, pointing this way and that, always leading to a place where that file and the unknown waited.

The chandeliers were dark. Entering the lobby behind her husband, Callie ran her fingers over the polished walnut, the fine brocades and silks. The cold smoothness of a chest inlaid with mother-of-pearl. The carpets sank silently under her slow steps. She knew she had to forget herself now and yield to the role she had cast for herself. There could be no turning back. She would do what had to be done.

It was clear almost from the beginning that he wasn't going to sleep—not right away, anyhow. And Callie, after having drunk so much champagne, was surprised at how clearly her mind was working. In the bedroom, they began undressing each other in a ritual of tenderness. Her evening dress was opened and she felt the wet warmth of his mouth through her chemise, then on her bare skin. From under her skirt he took her panties down, a wisp of white cotton with an edging of lace. A thrill trembled in her legs and her throat ached with things she wanted to say, but there were no words. With the thin metallic sound of a clasp, his trousers fell to the floor.

Callie laughed deliciously and lifted her lips close to his ear. "I'm a naughty girl tonight," she murmured and moved around behind him. With a rustle of clothing, she was naked, her gown fallen at her feet. She stepped out of her high heels and with a deft movement of her foot swept them aside. Her nipples stood out hard as rosebuds. "Be nice to me," she whispered, shivering. Her desire was real; she felt weak with want as he put her on the bed, her hair shifting over her shoulders in a scented wave. The silky smoothness of her thigh slid along his leg, her mouth breathed his name. Callie closed her eyes. His mouth came near her again; his lips closed upon her nipples. Her body gave itself; it opened softly to his swollen flesh and he came into her, all at once. The delicate musk of his body. Her soft, yielding defenseless flesh. No more doubt. No fear. Only ecstacy beyond words. If only the night could burn forever, she thought, like a dazzling red sun fanned by cosmic winds.

A long time later it seemed, she came

back to herself sobbing for breath on the large satin bed. She wanted to hold him, but her arms were weak and she remained where she was beside him, limp, feeling only the hammering of her own heart. "Christ," he muttered. "You wear me out."

"Me, too," she said. But then she opened her eyes and smiled at him. "Let's do it again."

He groaned and started to laugh, wearily. Lying next to him, she could see the moist sheen of his eyes in the near darkness. Now more than ever, Callie felt paralyzed; even their lovemaking had not prevented her fears from overtaking every sensation, every thought.

The state of Michigan versus Malcolm Preston Harwood . . .

What did you do, my darling?

An hour passed. Maybe longer. Her body was half asleep, but mentally she was wide awake, sensitive to his every breath. Only a few days ago the ghost of a happy couple had vowed before God to cherish and protect each other with a love that had seemed boundless, infinite. Now she lay waiting—waiting for the deep, even rhythm of his sleeping breath.

Through a slit in the drapes, the moon sent a gleaming blade of light that divided the room in half. Still, she waited. When she thought she could stand it no longer, Callie tried to look at her watch, but the dial was difficult to read in the slash of light and it made no difference anyway. Quietly, she stirred, raised herself on one elbow and leaned over him, lightly nuzzling his hair, the curve of her body fitted against him. For several seconds she watched him closely. He was adrift in the slow motion of his dreams, all the tension gone from his face.

If I'm going to do it, she thought, I have to do it now. With a light brush of her lips, she kissed his cheek and waited.

Malcolm didn't move.

It was a little after 4:15 when she slipped from the bed, drew on a negligee and went into the bathroom. Careful not to make a sound, she closed the door; unavoidably, the lock made a soft, buried thud as the bolt slid home. If he wanted in, Callie knew the lock wouldn't stop him, but it would definitely slow him down. And the noise alone would provide her with adequate warning.

The small bathroom was boxlike and

claustrophobic to start with; now with the door closed it was so dark that the air itself seemed to close around her and wait. Callie couldn't stop thinking: *Something awful's going to happen.*

Feeling through the dark, she located the fluorescent light above the mirror and flipped the toggle switch. A humming blue-white light blinked and came on. Irreproachably neat and smelling faintly of antiseptic, the room shrank back from her into its dimensions. Now a feeling of terrible urgency dogged her every move; Callie opened the cabinet doors below the sink and, with trepidation, withdrew the file from behind the spare six-pack of toilet tissue.

Her hands were trembling a little as she removed the thick rubber bands and cut the string from the file with her cuticle scissors. The bindings fell away. Using the counter next to the sink as a table, she drew a long nervous breath and opened the manila folder. All at once she stood straight and still. She could have sworn she heard the soft tread of a footstep on the other side of the door. She listened. No, it was nothing. Guilt, she thought, working on me.

Inside the folder, the pile of old papers

had yellowed at the edges, but the first thing on top was a brown 5 × 7 envelope. With her fingernails, Callie undid the small, metal clasp and opened the paper flap. A smell of musty age flew in her face as she pulled out the stack of photographs, ten or twelve of them, black and white glossies.

The first one was a police mug shot of a boy with numbers running across the bottom, a young boy, twelve, she guessed, or thirteen. My God, a child. It took only a moment for her to assimilate that it was Malcolm. Yes, she could see it. A young Malcolm. *Her Malcolm.* When he was just a boy. He looked terribly withdrawn and dark and frightened and there was a wild look in his eyes. But it was *Malcolm,* undeniably, a photograph of *him. What did you do?* It made her feel queasy and she didn't want to look at it any longer; she turned it over and put it away from her on the counter, face-down.

The next photograph slammed into her like a jolt of electricity: it was the picture of a body, a young woman's dead body lying in a pool of black blood. Her face was so torn and bloodied and anguished it was almost impossible to tell what she once had looked like.

Callie reached out and clutched at the towel rack to steady herself. *Oh, God.* Even with the stark black and white film, it was clear the woman had been horribly, viciously slashed with some kind of blade. It made Callie shudder and she felt disgust flowing through her like a searing pain. Bile filled her throat and for a moment she thought she was going to be sick; Callie clasped her hand over her mouth and then gulped air in an effort to stop it.

The second and third photographs were extreme close-ups of the same shot and they left no question that the woman was dead—her pitiful eyes, like a broken doll's eyes, were rolled halfway back and in one, because of a change in lighting, Callie could see that the wounds through her body had all but opened her up. And there was blood, speckles and splatters and puddles of blood. Everywhere.

The blue and ivory tiles of the bathroom dissolved under Callie's feet. For several seconds, she felt light-headed and had to keep her grasp on the towel rack. These were police photos, she realized, old police photos from some murder scene. But who was this woman? And what did it have to do with her? And with Malcolm?

Her hands were shaking so hard she could barely pinch the corners of the photos to turn them over, but she did and she looked at them, one after the other. And they were all roughly the same; they were all photographs of a murdered girl from different perspectives and angles, one more explicit and horrible than the next. The last two of them showed the partially clad body on a stretcher, but in the end it struck Callie that they were all very much the same. Who are you, Callie found herself thinking, who are you?

When she had finally leafed through them, Callie's face was damp with perspiration and she still felt horribly queasy. And yet, for her, there was something totally unreal about these grisly photographs; it was like a hard look at the savagery once depicted in old *True Detective* magazines, of the kind her grandfather kept around the house. Those had not seemed real, either, to the eyes of a ten-year-old.

As soon as she could get a grip on herself, Callie restacked the photographs, slid them into the envelope, closed the tiny metal clasp and put the envelope aside. Her hair was falling in her face; she picked up the silk ribbon she used when putting on makeup and tied her hair back, while her attention was riveted to the file and the pile of old papers it contained—papers that had yellowed at the edges. At a quick glance, they appeared to be an assortment of many different things: letters, procedural documents and parts of police files, hospital records and doctor's reports. But the first page was blank. And the second.

Then:

murder!

From among the arrangement of words, her eyes somehow snagged on that one word and immediately leapt to the top of the typewritten page.

On or about February 27 of this year, in the venue of Logan County, Michigan, MALCOLM P. HARWOOD, defendant herein, did commit murder in the first degree in that he did knowingly, intentionally and with malice aforethought trespass with force and arms upon the person of Millicent Satterfield, thereby taking the life of the afore-mentioned Millicent Satterfield.

Murder!

Even with all her doubts and suspicions, she had never thought . . . Malcolm! *Murder.* Oh, God, she didn't want to look at this, didn't want it to be true.

A series of letters and court documents followed, including reports and correspondence from various attorneys and physicians. Someone—Malcolm's father presumably—had dated the pages along with whatever typewritten date appeared on them. She came to a hospital report dated March 15: *". . . the admitting physician noted that the suspect, Harwood, had nothing to say and seemed to be in a state of shock, although clinically that could not be determined. When an effort was made to engage him in conversation, for example when asked if he had been taking drugs, he continued to be unresponsive. It was duly noted that he was detached and out of touch with his environment . . ."*

A letter dated April 9: *". . . Was he insane? It's possible that the only way Mal-*

colm could discharge the explosive rage and anxiety he had built up inside and re-store psychic order was through the most extreme violence. In my professional opinion, Malcolm Harwood killed his mother's secretary in an act of rage . . ."

The room seemed to recede, to grow dim. Callie had to close her eyes for a few seconds to stop the blue-white light from spinning. Again she wiped the perspiration from her face.

Keeping an apprehensive eye on the locked door, she tried to skim through the pages more quickly, but their sheer volume made it slow going. And she kept getting caught up in what they said. Shiver after shiver spread up her spine as the damning details continued to mount.

A letter from the law firm of Skaggs, Skaggs, Timmerman and Henning. June 23, 1983: *"This is a case of circumstantial evidence since no witnesses to the murder have come forward—indeed there apparently are no witnesses—and even though the boy showed detectives the murder weapon in his bed. Once the grand jury convenes, we will immediately move that the confession was obtained illegally and*

*should be stricken from the record, espe-
cially in consideration of the fact that the
defendant is a juvenile . . ."*

Murder weapon, she thought. Confession. Oh, Malcolm.

Twenty minutes passed, twenty minutes that seemed no more than a tick of a clock. She riffled through the pages with a doomed kind of foreknowledge pounding in her head. She did come across what appeared to be a police photograph of a butcher knife crusted with blood, which turned her stomach, but there was nothing that looked even vaguely like the transcript of a confession. So . . . she wondered, did that mean the attorney had been successful in suppressing it?

August 30: *". . . although Malcolm
may seem normal, his mental condition can
deteriorate to a psychotic 'state' in seconds
and vice versa. If, for example, he did commit a monstrous crime during one of these
'states,' he might conceive that he's done
nothing wrong. It would only be after the
fact when his mind returns to some sem-
blance of normal organization, that he
would either forget what he has done com-*

pletely or, if he remembers, find it as repre-hensible as everyone else."

Pressing her trembling fingers to her forehead, she tried to think what was she not seeing. Was there anything wrong with this? With her mind blank to everything except what was before her, she turned directly to the newspaper clippings in the back of the file. They were old; some of the edges crumbled and broke when she separated them.

KILLER KID ATTEMPTS SUICIDE

December 26:

An emergency medical team was summoned last night to the cell of alleged teenaged killer, Malcolm Harwood, where he had reportedly tried to commit suicide. As soon as he could be revived he was rushed by ambulance to Glasgow Memorial Hospital for treatment and observation . . .

FATHER'S GRUESOME TESTIMONY SHOCKS COURTROOM

January 9:

In a statement that shocked a packed courtroom, the father of accused murderer Malcolm Harwood admitted he was at the scene of the homicide. Called as a hostile witness in his son's grand jury hearing this afternoon, Preston W. Harwood described under oath the ghastly murder scene as he found it on the night of February 27, nearly a year ago.

Prosecutor William Jeffers placed a police photograph of the victim in front of Harwood as he asked about the occurrence. "How does it make you feel when you see that picture and know you were there at the time?"

"I'm sickened," said Harwood.

Callie came across a picture of Mr. Harwood, younger, sleeker, his dark hair combed straight back, accompanying his wife through a throng of reporters up a flight of steps, with the caption: WEALTHY PARENTS OF ACCUSED MURDERER ARRIVE AT COURTHOUSE. God have mercy, she thought. Don't let this be true. But the headlines and the photographs did not stop; there were many more.

BOY RULED INCOMPETENT FOR TRIAL IN SECRETARY'S SLAYING

January 30:

The tragic cycle that brought Malcolm P. Harwood, 14, to the grand jury on a murder charge came abruptly to an end this afternoon. Based on psychological evaluations, Logan County Circuit Court Judge John Frazier declared Harwood incompetent to stand trial for the February 27 slaying of Millicent A. Satterfield. Frazier ordered Harwood hospitalized for 180 days and recommended treatment at Dunbar State Hospital, which has a special unit for the criminally insane. Frazier added that, at the conclusion of the sentence, the case will be reviewed by the court.

"I feel I have no other choice," Frazier confided. According to experts, Harwood suffers from, "a very acute paranoid delusional system."

"He cannot understand the severity of the charges against him," said Dr. Theodore Trask . . .

Criminally insane, Callie thought and the two words became a litany stuck in her mind. There were printed photos of the accused taken into custody with his jacket covering his face, a badly yellowed picture of the aristocratic, Harwood "death" house, and one of the draped victim's body on a stretcher. A few of the articles had even shown diagrams of where and how the body had been discovered, including a minute-by-minute map of the alleged killer's apparent course of action.

One of the last clippings, dated fourteen months later, had appeared on page

A-8. It was brief, but in its simplicity, its finality, it was eloquent.

March 19, 1986:
. . . Judge Frazier said today he has released young Malcolm Harwood from Dunbar State Hospital into the custody of his father, industrialist Preston W. Harwood. He also said he has granted the fifteen-year-old six months probation. He declined to specify the terms of the release, except to say that the youth will be required to continue his psychiatric and drug therapy under state supervision.
The dead woman's parents, Mr. and Mrs. Ernest Satterfield, pleaded with Frazier to reconsider his ruling and to impose a more severe penalty, but Frazier said he has no power to withhold the boy's release . . .

Callie started going through them again. When a clipping consisted of two or three separate columns stapled together, she carefully picked them apart, looking at each individual piece of paper, until all of a sudden, she stopped, hand poised on the page. There it was! In the bleak fluorescent light she saw a face, a photograph of a face —a face of such rage and hatred that it seemed to lash out at her.

She almost dropped it.

It shook her like a blow.

The caption read: KID SLASHER GROWS UP— THE FACE OF A KILLER TRACKED DOWN IN MANITOBA. Last known snapshot of murderer, Malcolm Harwood.

It was Malcolm, probably at eighteen or nineteen; he appeared to be about the same age as he had been when she remembered him from the University of Michigan. His mouth was drawn back on his teeth; his eyes crazed with fury. The photographer had captured him in the act of throwing something at the camera, and the look on his face—the rage was unimaginable.

He was working at a logging mill, stripped to the waist, wearing gloves and a rolled bandanna around his neck, slathered with sweat and sawdust, a hard, strapping figure.

Bending down, Callie peered into the

face. It was Malcolm. No doubt. Unmistakable.

Maybe in some unconscious way she had known all along it was the face she would find. It told her what she had feared most—a truth she had strenuously resisted all night in her mind.

Recognition was followed by a hot flush of fright that made her heart thud. Malcolm, oh, Malcolm. Callie felt her body fill with an inexpressible anguish.

How could I have been so blind?

Emery had suspected there was something wrong with him. If only she'd paid more attention. Well, there was no use crying about that now. "But something should have told me he was bad," she moaned to herself. "Something should have told me."

She was completely unable to hold herself still. *What am I going to do?* Callie wrapped her arms tight around herself, shivering with fear.

She tried to finish reading the articles, in order to fix the words and sentences in her mind. She pressed her hands to her mouth struggling not to make a sound, while all over she felt minute pinpricks of pain.

"Callie?"

Her whole body leapt as though she had been whipped.

Suddenly a fist rapped the bathroom door.

"Callie?"

Panic surged into her throat, choking her to incoherence. He knocked a second time before she could manage to answer.

"Yes." She struggled to get her voice right. "Just a minute."

Hastily, she wiped the tears that had pooled in her eyes. She hadn't heard his approach; his voice, sharp and staccato, still reverberated through her.

"What's the matter? You all right?"

Her throat felt so dry, it was a few seconds before she could answer. "Yes, I'm coming."

All at once the doorknob jangled and again she flinched inside herself.

"Why did you lock the door? What's wrong?"

Only against the persistence of his voice was she able to pull herself together, her movements becoming automatic, her feelings numb. *Slasher! That girl's slashed body!* Her mind began to operate coldly;

she told herself she was stronger than she'd thought.

"I wasn't feeling well," Callie replied. Quickly, while still gazing at the door, she gathered the papers, jammed them into the file. She didn't see the clipping that fell loose. "But I'm all right now," she said. "I'm coming."

Moving fast, Callie replaced the file, along with the envelope of police photographs, in the battered manila folder and wrapped the cut string that once had held them, tightly around it. Now, where? *Where?*

Her eyes caught on the big, leather pouch of a purse she usually carried—the purse she'd left here earlier when she had been searching for the right lipstick. No one would go through her purse, least of all Malcolm. That's where she would put the file for now, until she could decide what to do with it. Callie pushed the file down into the big pouch and quietly closed the leather flap. Inches from her ear, his fist rapped the wood panel. Hard. *"Callie!"*

She stood and straightened the negligee on her shoulders, unlocked the door and bravely opened it, but her arms and legs felt heavy, filled with the leaden weight of fear.

He was standing on the other side in his shorts, leaning with one arm straight against the doorjamb. There was that face —she remembered the face of his rage. Her focus skipped past him through the darkness toward the doorway out, but all she could see was the streak of moonlight on the rumpled bedclothes, aglow like white phosphorescence. She couldn't bear to look at his face. In a practiced voice she might have used in a scene, she said, "Well, you didn't have to wake the entire hotel."

It was a few seconds before either of them spoke again and then they both spoke together. Finally he said, "Come over here, Callie." His face did nothing to dispel the menace. "Don't ever lock the door on me."

She looked around helplessly and nearly panicked; she felt caught, inextricably caught. I can't let him know, Callie thought. She took an abortive step toward him, then stopped. She was afraid to look at him directly, afraid she would give herself away.

"You've put your hair up," he said and smiled. "Why don't you undo it?"

How long had he been awake? she wondered. How much had he heard? Had he heard the papers rustling? It chilled her. Stop it, she thought. Stop it! Stop it! You've got to get a grip on reality. But she couldn't stop. Uncontrollably, her eyes traveled in the direction of her baggy purse and when she looked back, she realized his eyes had followed the same path.

With the cold uneasiness still gathering at the back of her mind, she saw him moving toward her. A feeling of alarm hung in the air; she was terrified. She did not stir when he reached out to untie the silk ribbon and yet it was as though she were succumbing to his desire. She didn't move. His fingers pulled the end of the silk; the ribbon fell and her hair tumbled about her face and shoulders. "There," he said, "now you look like yourself," and he kissed her.

Callie smiled nervously. Her overpowering impulse was for flight. Not to have to be here alone with him; not to have to try to fall asleep beside him. He came over to her and stopped a foot away. "Now take off the nightgown," Malcolm said.

Outside came the emptiness of the Pacific, the rush of waves breaking over rocks.

"Take it off, Callie," he said gently.

She couldn't answer. My God, he wants to make love to me. She kept staring at him. Her loosened hair shifted against her cheeks.

Don't say anything, she thought. Give in. She saw his hands reaching out, but she didn't have the strength to stop him. With his two hands, he grasped the straps of her negligee and with a swift motion pulled them down off her shoulders. She felt cold air strike her nipples as her breasts stood exposed. Backing away from her, he studied her appraisingly. Callie made no movement to return the straps to her shoulders. She stood facing him, staring at him.

"Gorgeous," he said. When Malcolm caressed her arm, a chill gathered and spread down her back. *Give in. Give in.* He took her face in his hands and kissed her face and lips. "Come back to bed," he whispered into her hair, and it only added to her anxiety. "Come on, fraidy cat, the night's almost over."

Callie felt cold. She knew, of course, exactly what was being asked of her, but the look she gave him was at once searching and cautious. "Not right now," she said.

The coldness dug in deeper along her spine.

Malcolm enclosed her waist and drew her to him; there was a moment when she started to pull away, but she didn't. The memory of his father's warning came flooding back to her, *Don't get him angry. Whatever you do, don't get him angry.*

His passion, the seeking of his lips for hers, seemed suddenly tawdry and unreal. "Not so hard," she muttered, "not so hard, oh, baby, please, you're hurting me! Whatever you want—but easy . . . easy." She was tired—deadly tired, deadly afraid. What courage she'd had earlier had fled. Callie knew her face was totally unmasked now, all fear and pleading. Still, she made not a sound as he carried her to bed, rose over her and knowingly entered her body.

Toward the end, a peculiar detachment came over her, a kind of supernatural acceptance. Was this how it was with that girl? The body, the black blood. Give in. Give in. Callie saw him only in the briefest fragments: a glimpse of tight-shut eyes and then darkness, a curve of bare shoulder and the thrusting and then darkness. It was not love, it was not beauty, to her mind it was not even the Malcolm she once had known.

An indefinable period of time passed before she felt him take his hands away, struggle sideways and slide from her. And she saw how strong and defined the back of his neck was, the muscled shoulders. *Like a murderer's,* Callie thought. How strong he was—he could crush her. Immediately, she tried to erase the thoughts from her mind but she couldn't. Now, as though she were seeing him clearly for the first time, she couldn't stop thinking how violent and dangerous he was.

She had no memory of Malcolm lying down beside her. With her head in the pillow, neither moving nor speaking, Callie lay rigid for a long time, pretending sleep. I'll get dressed now, she thought, and go. She'd have to open the closet door and get into the chest of drawers. What if he heard me? And it made him angry? What excuse could I give. *Don't worry, darling, I just felt like getting dressed. In the dark.* No, it would never work—she was forced to lie there until she could sneak away.

Once she dozed off and after a minute woke, biting back a scream because she had dreamed he was coming at her with a knife. I can't believe it, I can't believe it, she kept thinking.

Slowly the moon's pearl-white streak crept over her like the hand of a dial.

Callie was not aware that she had been sleeping but she must have been. Outside the night was ending, a pale light smoldering at the edges of the curtains. Malcolm's nearness, the warmth of his sleeping body did nothing for her now. Having him there only served to remind her that she would not be his for long. He had fallen asleep— how deep or how sound she couldn't tell.

Oh, Callie thought. Who are you? *What have I done?*

The face. The knife. That woman's dead body. She couldn't stop reliving it.

Callie extricated herself from under the dead weight of his arm and threw on a robe. There was only one thing that mattered to her now—she had to find a way to save herself. She went to the bureau where she had unpacked her things, drew the top drawer open without a sound and took out her address book. It was a little after six when she looked at her watch. Silently Callie straightened and turned her head; all around her the suite was quiet.

Malcolm didn't stir as she quietly went out and closed the bedroom door. Entering the living room, she pulled the drapes and the shadowless gray glimmer of early dawn washed over her. She looked outside. I'd love to get out of here, she thought. But under the robe, she was naked. Somehow all the hours and minutes had drained away. Far below a siren sank through the last dark trenches of night.

At the table behind one of the sofas, she took up the telephone, hit nine for a long distance operator and when the operator came on, she used her own calling card and gave the woman Kristen Connell's number.

Twisting the cord on her finger, she sat down on the sofa, her body shivering. She turned to look back over her shoulder. So far, so good.

At the other end of the line, the ringing stopped, the telephone clicked and Kristen's recorded voice said, "Sorry we missed you. Leave your number and we'll get right back to you. Pronto."

"Hello . . ." Callie said, her voice

hardly rising above a whisper. "Kristen, are you there?" She waited a beat, hoping her friend would pick up the phone. It was surprising how breathless she had become. "Kristen . . . it's me . . . Callie. Oh, why aren't you there?" Her words came tumbling out in a hoarse whisper. "Oh, please, Kristen—God, I'm sorry to be calling you like this—so early. But I—I need your help. Could you please meet me . . . meet me at . . ."

It dawned on her that she didn't know San Francisco well at all. She needed a landmark that would be easily accessible and that Kristen would immediately recognize. But where? Strange, the only thing she could think of was the woman, last night, who had been carrying the shopping bag. "Kristen, if you could please meet me at Ghirardelli Square," she continued in a low, strained voice, "at about . . . oh, God, I don't know, at about eleven o'clock . . . at the main entrance. God help me, Kristen, I hope you get this message . . ." She said this last on a soft, shuddering sob.

And hung up.

She felt betrayed by Malcolm and lost. With her knees drawn up, she put her head down on her arms and suddenly the horror and the loneliness that had been gathering and waiting came pouring in and she began to weep. She felt utterly defenseless and she hated it. He killed that woman, she thought. *He killed her.* Never before had she felt so alone. Or so trapped.

Quieted by her hands over her mouth, the sobbing went on, raw and ugly, jerking her body in spasms. Callie wept and wept. The long, sleepless night had left her with next to no physical reserve and her gnawing sense of claustrophobia kept twisting tighter and tighter. It was as if the past had smashed through all the beauty of her marriage. "God help me, God help me," were the only intelligible words that rose from her cupped hands.

It was after 6:30 before—exhausted—she slumped down on the bed beside him and shut her eyes, knowing there was no sleep in her.

Day Five—Morning
Ghirardelli Square

11

God, get me out of here.

At breakfast, Callie was silent and tense, unable to eat even half an English muffin or drink the small glass of orange juice she had ordered from room service. She felt as if she were stranded on a tightrope, well aware that the slightest mistake would be catastrophic. Don't think, she told herself. Just act.

Twice Malcolm asked if she was feeling all right, and each time Callie made an excuse. The first time she told him, "I didn't sleep very well," and tried to smile. "You kept me up all night." But when she picked up her water glass, she could feel her hand lightly shake and could hear her own ragged breath and wondered if he noticed. "I'm a little on edge this morning," she told him the second time he asked. "I don't know why. I'll be fine." Still, when he reached to take her hand, she moved it away.

Why was she so withdrawn, Malcolm asked, when only hours before she had been full of excitement and love? Callie shrugged, hardly able to look at him. Was it because she'd had too much to drink? he asked, but she slowly shook her head. And when he turned, reaching for the coffee pot on the server, she saw, again, the threatening strength of his shoulders. *Murderer,* she thought. *You killed her. You killed that woman.*

For all the tranquility surrounding her, Callie felt her restraint wound tight. It was all she could do to avoid looking through the open bathroom door toward her pouch purse containing the file, which still sat on the floor. While Malcolm refilled his coffee cup and went on with his breakfast, Callie was conscious of paying attention to even his most insignificant remark and she grew increasingly restless whenever he tried to touch her.

Already afraid of what she was going to do, she could hardly bear to sit still. All she wanted now was to get away from him, away from this marriage and back to the unpredictable world of moviemaking where she belonged. If she went now, went away somewhere, maybe eventually everything would be all right.

She had words on her lips, carefully prepared and calculated words, but for several minutes she didn't utter a syllable. Then she took a sip of her coffee, swallowed it and cleared her throat. *Get out! Get out!*

"Darling, I've been thinking," she said, at last, "I haven't even had a chance to buy you a present. What would you say if we were on our own this morning?"

He looked up at her from his tilted face. "Trying to get rid of me, eh?"

"No, Malcolm, I—"

He chuckled. "Come on, Callie, why're you so tense?" He was still amused with her. "To tell you the truth, you haven't been yourself all morning." He put his hand across the table and brushed his knuckles against the back of her fingers. "Maybe a change would do you good—why didn't you just tell me you needed a shopping fix?"

Even his attempt at tenderness and good humor chilled her, but she knew better than to resist. To resist was insanity.

"I'm sure there're things you'd like to do without me, too," she said, forcing a smile. "But it does sound like fun."

"Sure. Why not?"

She never knew how afterward, but she forced herself to remain seated across from him for another thirty seconds. Then with exaggerated casualness, she stood up. "I think I'll get dressed," she said.

"Fine," he said.

Callie stepped back and started across the room. In the bathroom her legs quit on her at last, but she managed to get the door closed before she slumped back against the linen closet. She couldn't hear anything above the hammering of her own heart. If Malcolm somehow put two and two together, she thought, she would have to remain calm, deny everything, and cooly claim that he was jumping to conclusions.

Coming out of the bathroom fifteen minutes later with her big pouch purse slung over her shoulder, Callie said she would shop for a couple of hours on her own, that she didn't want him with her while she rummaged around dress departments. Freshly made up, her hair tied back in a soft knot, she'd put on her sandals and a sleeveless dress cinched at the waist with a wide black belt.

"Don't forget your raincoat," he warned. "It's going to rain."

They arranged to meet for lunch at a restaurant in Union Square, near the corner of Geary and Powell Streets. Callie was a little surprised at how easy it was to deceive him. As if it were a matter of routine, she picked up her address book from the bureau and slipped it into her purse. He walked her to the door.

The living room was as silent as wreckage as she passed through it, the opal-colored orchid standing in its vase as if frozen in time. All at once it struck her that she was actually leaving and her fear could not suppress all the beautiful feelings she'd had for him. Unexpected tears filled her eyes. She felt for a moment as though she were abandoning her whole existence. Oh, dear God, she thought, I don't want to break down and cry.

Hastily, awkwardly, she bent forward to kiss him and say, "Bye," and to cradle his head—for the last time. She tried hard to think of something final to tell him, but only one thing came to mind that she knew to be the truth. "I'll never love anyone else," she said. "Not like this."

"Not in any way," he agreed.

When she tried to press by him, Malcolm reached out and took her hand. "Wait a minute," he said. Callie struggled slightly as he drew her in and then she forced herself to be still, to be nothing more than the lips that touched his. His fingers slid into her hair, drawing her close, his mouth meeting hers. "I don't want you to go," he said.

Oh, don't do this, she thought. Even these last moments with him were poisoned by the uneasy way her sense of danger grew. "Come on, darling," she said. "It'll do us both good."

Malcolm pulled her tightly against him and whispered he would always love her, but she drew back with a shiver and eased free of him.

"It's only a couple of hours," she said. In her wish to be gone, Callie caught only part of his good-bye and quickly shed his caress. She couldn't bear to stay with him any longer. She knew she had to get away or she would go insane with fear.

"Bye-bye," she said, determined not to let her voice quaver. "See you later."

Another step back. Back and away. *Away from him.* And another. *Away. Get away!*

Callie could feel Malcolm watching her as she went out and closed the door. But in the hallway, it took a moment for it to sink in that she had done it—she was alone.

Free.

She ran down the hall.

Yawning, Malcolm walked back into the bedroom to the breakfast table set for two, but he only picked at his food and looked at Callie's untouched plate. He scratched the back of his head, refilled his coffee cup and drank half of it, even though the coffee had lost its flavor. From outside came the raucous cries of gulls breaking the late morning stillness. It was 10:35. He rubbed his chin. He needed a shower and shave.

In the bathroom, humming to himself, he took a fresh towel from the linen closet and hung it on the rack outside the tub. Then he peeled the wrapper off a new bar of soap and put Callie's shampoo on the ledge beside the soap holder. His Gillette

razor needed a change of blades, he remembered; he was reaching to get one
from his Dopp kit on the back of the toilet,
when he noticed an old piece of paper lying
face-down behind the base of the stool.

He pulled the robe back onto his shoulders and reached down to pick it up. It was
a newspaper article.

What's this? he thought.

Then he saw his own face staring back
at him.

Callie rode down in the elevator, her light
raincoat shifting against her calves. When
she reached the first floor and got off, she
stood for a moment with her eyes shut and
eagerly breathed in the cool air of the lobby.
From somewhere she heard a door close
and it jarred her to hurry into the crowd, in-
tuitively putting on her sunglasses and tying
a scarf around her hair.

In tense haste, staring at the marble
floor and trying to be as inconspicuous as
possible, she crossed the lobby where bell-
boys in red livery were handling carts of luggage for the guests who were checking out.
Before she could stop herself, she collided
with a woman who was leaving.

"I'm so sorry," Callie said, self-consciously and quickly went on. Please don't recognize me, she prayed, please don't anyone recognize me. Keep going, she thought. Concentrate. But even so, her thoughts were incoherent. Inexpressible. Only one distinct memory remained of the night before. That rage, that face.

If she was being watched or followed, she preferred not to know it. And yet, she realized she was thinking of nothing else, and clenched up with panic every time someone brushed by her. Her nerves knotted at each approaching step and every shadow that fell across her path.

She had to get a cab, fast. Through the glass doors of the main entrance she could see the bellman—he would summon a cab for her. She could see the area under the canopy outside was crowded with departing guests but without any hesitation, she turned down along the bank of telephone booths, and practically ran toward the revolving doors.

A hard chill spread through Malcolm.

As if hypnotized, he gazed down at the printed photograph of himself. He had seen this same article before, two or three years ago. But where had this come from? It made no sense to him. Malcolm forced his eyes to read through the caption again. KID SLASHER . . . TRACKED DOWN IN MANITOBA—and he realized he was taking very shallow breaths, his body as tense as a wire. How did it get here?

The truth of what had happened began to seep in. *Callie,* he thought. It had to be Callie. Last night she had spent a lot of time in the bathroom; she'd stayed in there for nearly an hour. He remembered wondering what could be taking so long. At one point he had even listened at the door and no matter what she said, he hadn't heard anything that indicated she was sick.

It dawned on him now that when she came out, it was as though in some subtle way everything had changed, even her smallest responses to him had been out of kilter—but he had simply chalked it up to one of her moods.

Now she knows, he realized. *She knows all about me.*

A long hard ripple of desperation ran through him. That's why she had acted so edgy this morning. *My father.* Somehow or other his father had gotten to her—he must have given her this, and everything else. All at once, he stalked out of the bathroom, ripping and tearing the newspaper wildly in his hands until it had disintegrated into crumbling pieces and he let them fall through his fingers.

Goddamn you to hell! I'll kill you! I'll kill you!

Malcolm looked down and he was trembling uncontrollably. *I'm falling apart.* He couldn't think, couldn't make up his mind about anything. For a moment he was totally disoriented. His head was spinning. Why hadn't he picked up on her signals?

She's leaving me! He recognized it now: *She's run away from me!* That's what she had been telling him all morning, in everything she did.

"I can't let it happen," he muttered aloud to himself. "I've got to stop her—I've got to get her."

Callie pushed through the revolving door and stepped into the hubbub of passersby and departing guests. She was so completely in the grip of fear, she hadn't permitted herself to think about Malcolm until she had reached the sidewalk. But now with solid concrete under her, she began to trust in earnest that she had managed to get away.

She turned and looked behind her. No one was coming after her. She took a deep, shuddering breath.

Murderer!

She was aware that Malcolm's father might be waiting for her anywhere. What had he said? Something like: *I'll be around; I'll try to follow.* But she didn't want to see him either.

I've got to get to Kristen.

As she moved under the shade of the canopy, she thought she glimpsed a man's figure in a doorway on the other side of the street but when she looked closer to make certain, whoever it was had disappeared into the shadows. With a strange, tense feeling as though she could feel eyes burning into her, Callie waited until a couple had boarded a cab and then approached the bellman, tipped him a five and told him she needed a cab right away.

The bellman blew his whistle and lifted his hand to signal. A cab swung into the drive and the bellman opened the back door for her. Callie threw herself all in a heap onto the worn upholstery, her head swinging around to look back.

"Where to, Ma'am?" the cabbie asked and she told him and he said to her, "Ghirardelli, coming up." The bellman waited until she was safely settled before touching his cap, bidding her a beautiful day and closing her door.

I did it! she thought. *I did it! I did it!* It was pure triumph to feel this sensation of finality. Malcolm would never find her now. Oh, he would come after her. Of that she had no doubt. Callie tried to convince herself that maybe, if everything worked out, she would have nearly two hours lead time. And by then she would either be with Kristen or on a plane back to Los Angeles.

The cab pulled out from under the canopy into snarled traffic.

In a mad scramble, Malcolm pulled on his trousers and a shirt, stepped into shoes, stuffed his wallet, change and keys into his pocket, and ran out of the bedroom. He snatched up the telephone in the living room, pushed the button for the main desk and when the clerk came on, demanded that his car be brought around. Now. "It's an emergency," he said. He slammed the telephone into its cradle. His hands were cold with sweat and he wiped them on the seat of his trousers as he ran out of the suite and down the hall.

My father.

He was so full of hatred he waited at the elevator for a minute before it struck him that he was losing time, critical time, and he darted around and threw open the metal door to the service stairs. Taking three or four steps at a time, Malcolm flew down the staircase until he reached the first floor and hurried through the lobby. Wildly he studied the crowd, but Callie was nowhere to be seen.

Which way would she go?

He sprinted out under the wide canopy. The Mercedes wasn't there. He didn't have time to wait for it. He ran back, against the grain of the crowd to the bellman, slipped him a ten and asked if he had seen his wife, Callie McKenna.

"I put her in a cab a couple of minutes ago," the man said.

"Did she say where?"

"I think I heard her say Ghirardelli Square."

In front of the hotel, California Street was clogged with a sea of yellow taxis. None of them were moving.

Callie looked out her side window toward the hotel's canopy—still no Malcolm. She leaned forward. "I'll give you a twenty to get me out of here."

"Lady, look around. I'm no miracle worker."

He's coming. I know it, I know it.

Remnants of the grisly photographs still trailed across her memory like the unraveling of a evil dream and she felt giddy with dread at the thought of Malcolm finding her.

All at once it dawned on Malcolm that the taxis were at a standstill. He ran out from under the canopy into the bright blue-white glassiness of the sunlight. Malcolm groaned, and shielded his eyes until his sight began to adjust. He waded among the yellow cars, looking into the side windows, first to his left and then his right. "Sorry," he told the startled occupants, "excuse me."

He climbed on bumpers to get between cabs and the cabbies yelled at him, "Hey, get the hell off!"

Callie was here, somewhere, caught in traffic. Still nothing was moving. If only he could call to her, Malcolm thought, but he knew, if anything, it would only cause her to hide from him.

Desperately he went on, peering into windows. "Sorry . . . sorry," as the cabbies had started to honk their horns, one, then two of them, then six, then God only knew how many.

At the sunlit window of the hotel coffee shop on the ground floor, Harwood stood watching him. He followed Malcolm moving around and climbing over the cars and cabs, looking, searching. Slowly he turned his head. Ten or twelve cars farther up the street, he saw Callie stick her head out her cab window and look back, and she must have seen Malcolm because she instantly shrank back.

So she's seen it, Harwood thought, she read the file. He turned his head back toward Malcolm, and it was obvious that he had seen her, too, because he was now tearing through the tangle of cars—but like a log jam breaking loose, the traffic had started to move.

Harwood dropped a couple of bucks by his coffee cup on the counter and went quickly outside to his car.

Malcolm was getting closer. She saw him winding his way toward her and her fingers started tapping frantically on the edge of her seat. *Hurry up, move!*

He was six cars away.

Then five.

Then four.

He was drawing closer and closer.

"All right, here we go," the driver said.

Finally the cab surged forward and they were moving. Callie sank back in the seat, exhausted and with relief. Behind her sunglasses, her eyes closed momentarily. It was obvious even to her that the strain of the last twenty hours or so was telling on her. She was more tired than she had realized. She couldn't think straight, couldn't focus on anything except getting away from him as fast as possible.

She's getting away!

As he fought his way through the moving traffic, someone yelled at him or he would surely have been hit by a car. Horn blaring, the driver let out a stream of curses while Malcolm jolted back. He kept trying to keep his eyes pinned on Callie's cab, but was met by a barricade of passing cars. Then a panel truck rammed past, dragging giant red letters before his eyes. When it was gone, so was Callie.

It took him a minute or two to find a cab of his own.

"Where are we?" Callie asked.

"We're on Hyde, headed north."

"I've got to be there in about twelve minutes. Can we make it?"

The driver chuckled and shrugged. "I'll do what I can," he said.

Callie rocked with the motion of the cab.

They hadn't traveled very far when the driver said, "We've got construction on Larkin, so I'll just go down here on Hyde to cross over. That okay with you?"

"Yes," she answered, "yes . . . whatever. Just get me there."

Callie settled back against the seat with her left forearm pressed against her opened mouth while tears welled up in her eyes. She didn't want to think about anything anymore. She wanted just to live, to deaden her senses, to fill her days with empty, meaningless pastimes.

When the taxi finally stopped at the corner of Beach and Larkin Streets, it was 11:03 and Callie was already half out of the cab. The meter showed a charge of $7.35; she pushed a ten to the driver, slipped out and slammed the door. Five seconds later she thought she heard another car door slam, but she didn't look around. She was already across the sidewalk and up the three zigzag flights of steps.

All of a sudden, she felt in her purse for the manila file. It was still there. Get rid of it, she suddenly thought. I can't let Malcolm find it. Get rid of the damned thing once and for all. At the first trash container she came to, Callie dumped the entire file into it. Then she closed the leather flap of her purse, returned it to her shoulder and rushed on.

Ghirardelli Square was not quite what she had pictured. It was an open plaza on differing levels, hemmed in on all four sides by galleries and cafés and shops. Along the back ran the rustic chocolate factory and belfry. At a little past eleven, the promenade was thronged with tourists. Not far from the entrance, Callie turned on her toes, searching the crowd for Kristen Connell's familiar face. But no one even resembling Kristen met her gaze. Maybe she wasn't coming. Callie whipped around and ran up to the second level toward the fountain, her eyes still sorting through the milling crowd.

Suddenly, behind her, she thought she heard Malcolm's voice yell, "Callie," and she had to force herself not to turn around. She ran faster, while still trying not to attract attention, but she could feel him gaining behind her. Unable to gather her thoughts, she tried to continue to run even faster. It was no use, he was certain to catch her.

The footsteps drew closer—and a urgent voice called out, "Callie!" It was a voice she knew she couldn't heed.

Malcolm appeared from nowhere in the crowd behind her. His hand reached out and caught her forearm in a grip that made her wince. And her expression froze. He almost ran into her, she had stopped so suddenly. Malcolm's face was ashen, his forehead glistened with perspiration.

"What are you doing, Callie?" he said. "My God! I told you . . . I swear to God, you don't know what you're doing." His own voice broke with emotion and anger. His grip was like iron; she struggled trying to break his hold. And couldn't. "Don't you dare," he warned, his eyes aflame with anger. "Where d'you think you're going?"

"Nowhere. Let go of me."

"Don't make a scene here," he said.

"Let go of me, I said. I know everything. I'll scream."

Suddenly he backed her against the wall, all but hiding her from sight, and his hand was on her throat, throttling her. Rage slid into his eyes. "Don't," he said with a control that was eerie. "You don't know what I've been through. I'll never be locked up again. You know too much, but you know nothing. My father did this—he got to you, didn't he?"

Callie felt the pure cold blast of his hatred pass over her. In reflex, without thinking, she twisted and stepped out of his grasp and broke away. But before she could make a move to get away, he grabbed her and pulled her to him. "Don't do it," he said. "I swear to God, Callie, don't try anything else or so help me, I'll . . ."

"You'll what, Malcolm?" she gasped rubbing her throat. She coughed; there was a gagging in her voice. "You'll what . . . Kill me?"

It was almost as if she had slapped him. "You're just like him," he said. And then suddenly—

"Oh, there you are!" a voice exclaimed.

Surprise kept all three of them momentarily silent.

"Kristen!" Callie gasped.

"Callie! My God, Callie, I've been looking all over for you!"

In the crowd, Kristen Connell was hardly more than six feet away.

"Kristen! Oh, Kristen, you heard me, you got my call."

Malcolm was stunned. He stood as straight as a slab, his features impassive; his face was whiter and colder than she had ever seen it. Abruptly he leaned to Callie, his back half-turned to her friend. "Don't say anything," he said. "If you do, you'll wish you hadn't. I don't want to hurt you. Or her. Get rid of her."

But she was coming toward them. All of a sudden Callie broke from him and ran the few steps to her and they embraced. "Oh, Kristen, oh, God, I'm so glad . . ." Callie was choked up, unable to speak.

"I know," Kristen said. "I know." Her eyes softened sympathetically, the beginnings of an unhappy little smile worked at the corners of her mouth. "Callie, Callie, it's so terrible. I'm so awfully sorry." She was holding her, patting and rubbing her back.

"What do you mean?"

"You mean you don't know?"

"What?"

"Your friends, the Hudsons. They're dead."

"Dead? *Dead?* What're you talking about?"

"Haven't you seen the papers?" and Kristen held up the morning *Chronicle.*

Silence. Callie just stared at her. "Kristen, I . . . please, let me see that?" She reached out and took the newspaper from Kristen's hand.

"I don't know if you should; it's horrible. I'm glad you called. You're so lucky. Oh, Malcolm, what a joy that she has you."

But Callie hardly heard her. Above the fold, a one-column story riveted her eyes. BODIES RECOVERED, the small headline said.

Hollywood Producer and Wife Found Slain . . .

Kristen was saying, "I thought when I heard your voice . . . My friend, my oldest, dearest friend. I can't tell you how glad I am to be here for you."

Callie couldn't move. All over her body she felt minute pinpricks of pain. She was holding the newspaper so tight her hands were beginning to shake.

Dully, unable to absorb it at first, Callie found herself reading the words a second time:

BODIES RECOVERED

Hollywood Producer and Wife
Found Slain in Lake Arrowhead

The badly decomposed bodies of Emery V. Hudson, 66, and his wife, Dorothy Munro Hudson,

62, were found drowned Saturday night at their Lake Arrowhead estate. A police spokesman said a search for the couple had been ongoing since they failed to arrive at a meeting held in New Orleans last week. The bodies, sighted by children in the neighborhood, had been in the water for several days. Evidence at the scene suggests the possibility of foul play.

Longtime residents of this exclusive enclave were shocked . . .

"Oh, God," Callie moaned. "They're dead."

She continued reading every word and then tried to start reading it again. But a terrible, tingling panic ripped down through her legs.

"Oh, Kristen . . ." she began, then her mouth quivered; no longer able to control herself, a great wail of terror and grief tore from her lips. The plaza shifted unexpectedly before her eyes, her knees stiffened, and she had to catch hold of Malcolm to keep from falling. Tears appeared below her sunglasses. Her mouth was deathly pale.

All at once her sunglasses clattered to the concrete and she began to sob. The light came at her from every angle, shimmering off the glass windows and white walls. She slumped heavily against Malcolm; she felt weak and helpless, too weak to move.

Then Malcolm was saying, "It's all right, Callie, I'm here. I've got you."

"And I'm here, sweetie," Kristen said. "I'm here."

But when Callie opened her eyes, the shop windows reeled around her. They're dead, they're dead, reverberated from every side. Still in shock, she tried to shove them off. "All right . . ." she sputtered, "I'm all right." Then her knees buckled and she went down as if she'd been hit with a hammer.

She didn't know how much time passed; she was only half-aware of Kristen continuing to speak to her. "Here, take these," she said, and placed two capsules in Callie's mouth. "You'll feel better if you can rest." And when Callie tried to ask what it was, Kristen said, "Valium, they'll help you," as she washed them down with water from a paper cup. Callie felt herself sway as the first wave of medication hit her. The street danced before her eyes. Kristen put her arm around her shoulder and she was helping her, walking with her, telling her not to worry, "We're here, sweetie, we're here."

When Malcolm lifted her up in his arms, her head fell back. The milling crowd parted to let them through. It was then that Harwood saw them. He was standing at the edge of the fountain, on the other side of a rowdy group of third graders on a field trip. His eyes never left Malcolm and Callie and the other young woman with dark hair. Wait for them, he thought, see where they go. He knew he could do nothing in this crowd.

Staying a step behind Kristen, Malcolm carried his wife into the elevator and the lighted arrow indicated that they were going down. The garage, Harwood thought, they're going to her friend's car. And he began to move, fighting his way through the crowd, toward the street where his own car was waiting at the curb.

Kristen led them to a red Jaguar convertible sitting in the gloom with its top down. Gently, Malcolm put Callie into the backseat and got in beside her. "Is she okay?" Kristen asked, sliding behind the wheel.

"Yes," he said. It was only after he breathed once or twice that he was able to summon his voice. "We're fine back here. But—listen, we'd better get out of here, because the cops're going to come. We don't want a crowd, don't want this in the tabloids. We've got to move it."

"You're right. I'll take care of it," Kristen said, pausing at the pay window. "Hold on." With a shifting of gears, the red Jaguar tore out of the garage, swerved, straightened and shot due west.

They spun onto Bay Street on a snarl of tires; people looked up, startled, at the slim young woman behind the wheel, while stopped at a traffic light half a block back, Harwood stood outside the driver's door of his car, trying to follow their direction through his binoculars. "That's them," he said to himself. "There they go."

He got into the Mercury and threw the glasses on the passenger seat beside him. When the light failed to change, and it became more and more certain that he would lose them, Harwood twisted the wheel hard to the left, veered out from behind an Oldsmobile into the opposing lane and floored it.

Oncoming cars honked and darted

toward the curb in panic. Desperately he maneuvered past the slower traffic in an accelerating blur and blasted past Ghirardelli Square. At the intersection, he was forced to brake momentarily until there was a gap in the traffic. Almost a full city block ahead, he could see the red, low-slung shape of the Jaguar twisting in and out between cars.

In ten blocks, Kristen hit Cervantes Boulevard driving as fast as she dared through the crowded, noonday streets toward the Pacific and the great span of the bridge gleaming in the sun. The light was so bright and crystalline that it shone in Callie's hair like a sparkling crown.

Holding her to him, Malcolm looked down at Kristen's newspaper that he had managed to scoop up with Callie and bring along. Despite the bumps and jolts breaking his focus, he scanned as much of the article as he could.

Nothing. *Evidence at the scene suggests the possibility of foul play.* But no clues were mentioned. No fingerprints, no suspects.

• ⦿ •

Bay Street became Cervantes and then forked at Fillmore where a red light stopped Harwood. So they had veered to the right, he realized. Otherwise he probably could have seen them. He was all set to run the light when a police cruiser pulled up in the lane next to him. He looked over at the cop and the cop looked straight back at him through mirror sunglasses.

Harwood waited. He waited. Finally the light changed, but he was forced to go slowly. He drove to Marina Boulevard where he took a chance and burned left toward Highway 101 and the Golden Gate Bridge.

Even looking through the binoculars, he couldn't find them in front of him. But he was certain they had taken the bridge—it was the only thing that made sense.

Harwood hit the bridge with his horn blaring, pushed the accelerator up to 75. He lurched into traffic on the northbound lane and fought his way to the outside where fewer cars were traveling. *"Christ!"* he said and smacked the steering wheel hard. In rapid succession he passed two cars and nearly sideswiped a third. A horn blared at him like a scream falling through the air. He came off the bridge and eased back on his speed, searching the lanes in front of him.

Where had they gone? The red Jaguar was nowhere to be seen.

Again he accelerated. The needle twitching at 80, he drove for another ten miles and found no trace of them. But how could they disappear? Had they pulled off —toward Sausalito?

At the next ramp, he pulled off and brought his speed down to 40, then to 35.

They were gone.

I've passed them, he thought.

Violently, he jerked the wheel and brought the Mercury through the underpass and headed back the way he had come.

12

When they had driven out of Sausalito, Kristen said, "Now talk to me . . . you've got to let me help. We have a beautiful cottage . . . perfect for you. Just say the word and I'll give the housekeeper a call to get it ready."

"You've done plenty, Kristen, believe me," Malcolm told her. "We just had to get the hell out of there . . ."

"But you've got to let me do this for Callie. You'll hurt my feelings if you don't. You know what they say about missed opportunities. Sure, it's your honeymoon, but you can have the run of the house—you'll be entirely on your own. What do you say?"

The last thing Malcolm wanted was to have other people around. But he saw that he had no choice. Once they were hidden away at Kristen's, he'd have to find a way to handle Callie and that was all there was to it. "Sounds perfect," he answered.

"Then it's settled." Kristen smiled, her blue eyes mercurial, soft with light. "I'd planned to have a few people over for dinner, but I'll call and cancel—"

"No, come on, Kristen, neither one of us would want you to. We'll stay completely out of your way."

"Sweetie, you couldn't be in my way if you tried. I can't entertain now—not with Callie like this. I'm not that nutty." She laughed, picked up the car phone and called her housekeeper to prepare the cottage.

They turned onto Panoramic Highway toward Muir Woods and Mount Tamalpais, headed north. From time to time, Malcolm looked behind them, but for miles now no one was chasing after them. As the Jaguar moved though the curves, the highway rose gradually along cliffs. They followed a tortuous route, as if riding the sheer edge of oblivion. Across the narrow strip of pavement, the cliffs fell precipitously to the ocean.

The hour, the startling openness of the sky and the Pacific, the feeling of unexpected release did nothing to improve his state of mind. *She knows all about me.* When they rounded the next curve, Kristen pointed to a strip of land that jutted into the Pacific like a sandbar. "That's Bolinas," she told him. "We live near there." Looking out, the water was shimmering amethyst extending to a horizon that was layered in shades of blue-violet. Even as troubled as he was, he had to admit it was breathtaking to behold.

Kristen had to stop in Bolinas, she said, to get gas and to cancel a couple of orders she had placed and in a few minutes they pulled up beside gas pumps outside a coffee shop called Ambrosetti's. "I'll stay here with Callie," he said and she nodded and said she wouldn't be a minute. While the attendant filled the tank and cleaned the windshield, Kristen ran across the street to a bakery. Malcolm noticed the kid staring at Callie and considered shooing him away, but Kristen was coming back and the kid stopped scrubbing the glass with his paper towel. "Thank you, Miss Connell," he said, taking the bills she handed him.

Five or ten minutes later, they turned in at a cluster of mailboxes and after a crook in the road, followed a lane laid straight between sentinel pines where the air breathed deep of scented freshness. The place seemed as remote and safe as a country refuge. This couldn't be better, Malcolm thought; at least he had the satisfaction of knowing that it would be next to impossible for his father to find them in a private home.

A pair of soaring hawks hovered overhead, watching over them. What will she do when she wakes up? he thought. What will she say? On the drive, Kristen pulled up and parked the Jaguar at the side of the guest cottage. Sitting on the cove fifty yards away, the main house was bone-white, contemporary.

"Let me show you where you'll be," Kristen said as Malcolm gathered Callie up in his arms. She led the way around to the front of the cottage. "You can stay here as long you'd like . . . and let Callie get plenty of rest."

"Yes," he said.

Mrs. Quinn, the housekeeper, met them at the door and held it open for Malcolm to pass with Callie; Manuel, the gardener, who had been tending the eucalyptus, stood by ready to assist them. "What a terrible thing to have happen on your honeymoon. But never fear—she'll awaken soon. She'll be fine tomorrow."

The guest quarters consisted of a sitting room with a sofa, wicker chairs, a desk and liquor cabinet, a bedroom with a large turned-down bed, where he gently laid Callie, and an adjoining bath. "Let her sleep," Kristen said. "Those Valium were potent. If Callie's not used to them, she may sleep for hours."

Although small, the rooms were skillfully laid out, one evolving gracefully into the next. "Mrs. Quinn, would you mind getting one of my nightgowns from the house for Callie?" Kristen asked, and the housekeeper departed. On a small table by the bed stood a vase of fresh zinnias and snapdragons. Lamps and tables, rows of books on shelves and old framed prints were everywhere. Two large windows in the front provided a view of the swimming pool and, farther out, the main house and the Pacific.

"It's terrific here," Malcolm said.

"I hope you'll feel at home. But Malcolm, I'm worried about your things. Everything happened so fast, we didn't have time to do that."

"It's all right. I'll call the hotel and have them send them along." But not now, he thought, not for a day or two or maybe longer, knowing he couldn't provide anyone with a means of tracing them.

"Until then, there's extra toothbrushes and a disposable razor in the bathroom. Also some guest bathrobes. Please feel free to use whatever you need."

The housekeeper reappeared with one of Kristen's nightgowns. While the two women changed Callie's clothes, he bathed his face in cool water in the bathroom and wiped it dry. God, don't let them wake her up, he thought. As he came out a couple of minutes later, he heard Kristen asking Mrs. Quinn if she'd had any calls. Among the messages, a Bill Baudin had called, wanting her to call back. "He owns the place," Kristen laughed in telling him. "Absolutely cannot live without me."

He grinned and walked through the cottage, stepped outside and looked at the Jaguar. No one else was there. Malcolm let out his held breath. He had to get used to it, accept it. So far, everything was fine.

When he went back inside, Callie was clad in the borrowed gown, Mrs. Quinn was

leaving and Kristen was sitting on the side
of the bed, talking on the telephone. "Oh,
Billy, why didn't you tell me?" she said.
"That's so sweet." Casually, the conversation went on, her voice kept low. But Malcolm was only half listening. He leaned over
Callie, smoothing away a strand of her hair
that had fallen across her face, testing her
forehead for temperature.

"Me, too . . ." Kristen said, getting
off. "Yes, I will, I will, I promise, you too,
bye-bye, Billy. Bye." She put the phone
down.

"I don't know about you," Kristen said,
"but first things first and the first thing I
need is a stiff drink."

"Thanks, but I'll pass this time," Malcolm told her, as she went to the liquor cabinet in the sitting room and poured straight
bourbon into a shot glass. She raised the
glass, looking at him with remarkably blue
eyes. "Well, Mr. Rhodes, welcome," she
said. "Here's to you and my favorite old
married lady. I know she'll be all right; it was
a terrible blow. I'm glad the two of you are
here where I can look after you. Many,
many cheers."

She drank the way she did everything

else, fast, one right after the other. She swallowed two quick shots, then she was saying something about the dinner she was canceling. "I have some calls to make, so I'm going to leave you to it. If you need anything at all, just yell. I'll have the cook rustle us some food and I'll bring you a tray."

"That would be fine," Malcolm said.

"We should let Callie sleep."

When she had gone, Malcolm closed and locked the door behind her and leaned back against it. Beyond the lacy white pillows, the antique headboard of the bed curved protectively around Callie like a concave shield. She was limp with sleep. Malcolm realized how tired he was, too, and he had a headache, but he could find no name for the sudden despair that filled his heart. My father. *My father.* What other lengths would he go to? Now she knows, and she's going to wake up.

He took a long, hot shower, as hot as he could stand it, followed by an equally cold one; he shaved with care and combed his hair, glancing now and then through the open door toward the bed where Callie lay sound asleep. Wrapped in a terrycloth robe, he lay back across the bed next to his wife. He was in no hurry now.

Malcolm knew it was only a matter of time. So little time. And then she would awaken and remember what she had read about him, everything about him. He could think of no way to stop it. And he knew what had to be done, what life had dealt him. He accepted it now without fear, like a man standing upon a trap door. For all his love and for all hers, their life together had lasted no longer than the evil spell that followed him wherever he went. *You're mine now, only mine.* He loved her, but he had loved someone too much before and was betrayed. He kissed the tracks of her dry tears as if they were scars. Flesh of my flesh, he thought, blood of my blood.

13

An ancient grapevine grew up over the open roof beams, casting the terrace in shadow as deep and cool as a mountain hideaway. Night had fallen; the rim of the moon stood in the east, concentrating its red glow on the water as if it were burning.

It was nearly eight before Kristen crossed the terrace and made her way past the swimming pool, taking a dinner tray to the cottage. When Malcolm answered the door, she said, "If I'm disturbing anything, send me away."

He smiled. "No, not much is happening here. I was reading. Come in."

"How's our baby? How's she doing?"

"Fast asleep," Malcolm told her. "She's hardly moved."

"I brought you some dinner—I'm sorry it took so long." As she stepped inside, Malcolm took the tray from her and put it on the table where a open book lay facedown to mark his page.

"I've been tied up on the phone," she continued, "you know how it is. You've got to be hungry."

"I'm beginning to be. This's really thoughtful of you."

"If you don't mind, I'll just stick my head in for a minute," Kristen said.

He nodded.

Staying back, Malcolm followed behind her to the bedroom doorway and remained there, leaning against the door frame as she walked toward the bed. Only a small lamp was burning on a nearby table, casting a soft ray over Callie's hair. Kristen lifted her friend's hand in her own and rubbed it gently. "It's all right, sweetie; everything's all right. I'm here."

But there was no reaction at all. Still Kristen continued lightly stroking her hand for another few minutes. It was when she started to let go and return Callie's hand to the coverlet that Callie groaned, her fingers closing feebly on Kristen's.

In the doorway, Malcolm straightened and took a precautionary step forward. Callie seemed to be trying to speak. But there was nothing he could do.

A sound came from Callie's mouth: "Krisss," she seemed to say but it was little more than the air of sleep against the roof of her mouth. All at once, she grabbed her covers and twisted onto her side, away from them, and nestled back to sleep.

Kristen rose from the side of the bed and turned to Malcolm. "I'm glad you're here," she said. "I thought she was going to say something, but she'll probably sleep through the night. It'll still be hard on her when she wakes up."

"I'm glad we're here, too," Malcolm told her. "She's lucky to have you."

"Well, I should get back. Things will sort themselves out tomorrow."

He opened the door for her.

"Enjoy your dinner," she said.

"Thank you," he replied.

With a last look over her shoulder, Kristen walked back across the lawn. The small outdoor lights had come on, lighting the drive, the sidewalk, and the front of the house.

● ● ●

Malcolm watched as she dwindled from sight and then he stepped back inside, closed the door and locked it. The smile fell off his face; and the muscles in his jaws drew hard as iron.

How many times is she going to come over here? he thought. He began to drive his fist into his hand and rub and grind it in, like a stone in a mortar. She won't keep quiet. She's going to wake up. Kristen will know, too. He was roaming around the cottage, unable to sort the jumble of his thoughts. I'm trapped. I've got to get out of here. This can't happen. I can't let this happen. She'll tell Kristen. And he's out there somewhere, on his way. I've got to get out . . .

He couldn't eat, he wanted to throw that damned tray in the fireplace. Time after time, he picked up a book or a magazine and struggled to focus on the print, anything to break the flurry of his thoughts. But it didn't work; he couldn't concentrate for more than ten seconds.

Malcolm went to the edge of the drapes and quickly looked out toward the main house. She had put the car up; the garage was closed. Another dead end.

Even if he could somehow manage to take the car, when Kristen found it gone, she would report it missing and he would be picked up.

Time was passing, running rapidly through his fingers. *I'm losing it, I'm losing everything.*

The crickets had started in the surrounding trees, a racket that would go on most of the night. They lived only five miles out of town, but at moments like this Kristen felt keenly how isolated they were on this cove.

In the kitchen, the housekeeper said, "I'm all finished, Ms. Kristen."

"That's fine, Mrs. Quinn, why don't you run along?"

"I believe I will, if it's all right. Are you expecting Mr. Baudin to get back this evening?"

"Yes. He should be here any time now."

"So—when do you want me?"

"Oh, after the weekend. Monday's fine."

"Very well. I hope your friend's all right."

"She will be. Good night."

A few minutes later, Kristen listened as the woman's aged Honda pulled out of the drive.

She checked the doors to make sure they were locked, turned out the kitchen lights and started upstairs when she decided she was hungry after all. And in an hour or so she could catch the early evening news on TV.

Taking a platter of mushroom chicken and a plastic bag of salad from the refrigerator and a bottle of Henri Bourgeois Chenin Blanc from the rack, she created a quick and remarkably pleasant dinner for herself, even if tonight she was preoccupied. But she couldn't help it. Her thoughts did not stray for long from the cottage on the other side of the swimming pool.

Harwood kept to the main roads through Sausalito and Marin City, stopping at gas stations, showing photographs of them, working his way north. "Have you seen this girl?" he asked the attendants who came out. "She's riding in a red Jaguar convertible with a man and another woman."

"No," they said, shrugging their shoulders and shaking their heads, "sorry, no."

"Look closer," he urged. "You've probably heard of her; she's an actress, Callie McKenna. If you saw her, you'd remember."

But he got nowhere. He followed Route 101 and then picked up Route 1. After several miles, the road forked and he had turned left toward Stinson Beach, when he saw that the road was temporarily closed past Muir Beach due to the earthquake.

Up ahead, he could see workmen removing boulders with a backhoe and bulldozer and he pulled off to the side, parked his car and started toward them, when he saw one of the men break from his group and come forward.

"I'm the foreman here," the man said. "You can't come through here."

"I'm looking for this girl," Harwood said, handing him Callie's publicity photo. "She's in a red Jaguar convertible."

The foreman looked at the photo for several seconds and shook his head. "There was a red Jaguar come by here three or four hours ago. She's by here all the time. The reason I know is because she pitched a holy bitch when we had to close this road. Claimed it took her thirty miles

out of her way. I think she lives over around
Bolinas somewhere.''

"What's her name?''

"I can't say I remember—sorry I can't
help you.''

Bolinas was one of those coastal towns
that hadn't changed appreciably in several
generations. Its old storefronts had been
taken over by a motley of arts and crafts
boutiques and hole-in-the-wall restaurants.
On one corner sat a general store closed for
the night; an old schoolhouse could be
seen with a bell housing on the roof peak,
and a small white steepled church shone
bright with dew in Harwood's headlights.

At 10:18, the only lighted building was
a coffee shop with a couple of gas pumps
in front and its name, AMBROSETTI'S, etched in
red neon across the darkness. The placard
in the window said the place was open, but
it looked deserted as he pulled to the curb
and parked.

Exhausted and worried, Harwood entered Ambrosetti's coffee shop. A 10:30
closing time was posted on the door, and
except for a couple of teenage boys in a
back booth the place was empty. He took a

stool down the line from the cash register. A radio was playing behind the counter, tuned low to an oldies-but-goodies station, the melody soft, the beat persistent.

A waitress, who looked seventeen, came over to him, a blonde with a delicate face and body. He opened the thumb-worn menu and ordered a chicken salad on wheat. "Don't toast it." And a cup of coffee. Black. He flattened the newspaper and opened it. "And maybe a piece of pie. I'll let you know when I decide."

When she brought the coffee, he asked if she knew of the actress Callie McKenna and she said, "Yeah, I guess so." He showed her a publicity photo of Callie and a copy of the last snapshot he had of Malcolm and asked if they had been in. "Actually I was supposed to meet them here," Harwood said, nodding toward the sidewalk outside.

The waitress frowned, trying to think; she was pretty standing there in her tight white apron tied snugly around her. He noticed that she was chewing gum and she glanced up at the clock and then toward the boys in the back booth. Finally she gave him a blank look and told him that she didn't guess she had seen them, but she had only come on at six, as a favor for one of the other girls.

Harwood shrugged as if he understood. "My tough luck," he said. Another teenager came in and she had to go see what he wanted. Harwood half-expected her to return to him, but she didn't. He thought if he could continue to talk to her, he still might get some worthwhile information. He knew these girls didn't make much money, so he put a five-dollar bill under the edge of his saucer. He would tell her to keep the change when she returned with the coffee pot.

His sandwich arrived, a pickle and potato chips on the side. He cleaned his plate and hardly tasted it, then took his time finishing the coffee, knowing that it was time to get back on the road. The thought depressed and angered him. *They've got to be around here somewhere.* He looked out through the windows at the little town—it was like a lost settlement at the end of the world. Only one road led in, only one road led out. So how could they vanish like that? *Where the hell are they? This is my last chance—I don't know where to go from* here. Harwood turned back from the window when he thought the waitress was returning to him, but she went behind the partition in back with another order.

He sipped the hot coffee, silently. He hadn't eaten since breakfast and he felt a little better. Some of his pretense at good humor had abandoned him and he now felt the chill of the night's solitude. He didn't want to drive away and not know where he was going. Through the trickle of music on the damned radio, he could hear the waitress talking to the cook behind the partition and he struggled to overhear what was being said. He picked up his coffee cup and moved down a few stools to be more in line with the direction their voices were coming from.

"Yeah," the cook was saying, "they were getting gas. Jimmy comes running in, jabbering about guess who I just saw. It was her, he says—Callie McKenna, the one in the movies—you know, she played that girl Lottie, remember? She was out there in Kristen Connell's Jaguar with some guy, but she didn't get out of the car. That's what Jimmy said. He said she was asleep . . ."

"Hey, mister," the waitress said, sauntering out a couple of minutes later with the pot of coffee. "I think I know where they went."

But the counter was deserted.

"Sweetheart, this has to be quick. I'm in a phone booth. This is it. I'm closing in."

"Be careful. Preston, be careful."

Evelyn Harwood let the receiver fall back into its cradle and she was up out of bed, moving around the room, pacing first in one direction and then another. "My God," she muttered, "oh, my God."

Vivian had come in, locking the door behind her. "What's this now?" she said, in her gentlest, coaxing voice. "No, now, Miss Evelyn, come on, no more of this."

But it was as if Evelyn couldn't hear her. "I've got to go to him," she was saying, "I've got to go to him. He's in trouble; he's going to be in trouble." All at once, she stopped pacing. "What're you doing in here? Get out! Get out of here!"

"I brought your sleeping pill, Miss Evelyn," Vivian said, "that's all," but seeing the woman's wrath she put the small tray down. When Evelyn Harwood resumed her pacing, the black nurse quickly unlocked the door and retrieved her small black bag from her place outside. Again turning the lock behind her, she prepared a hypodermic syringe with sedative. "It's all right, Miss Evelyn," she said moving toward her without hesitation. "It'll be all right. Don't you do anything now. Come lie down."

Evelyn's strength was surprising. "No, it's not all right; things are not all right."

Vivian could hardly control her. Evelyn twisted out of her grasp and slapped the syringe out of her hand so that it went flying.

"Now look what've you done. Look there, Miss Evelyn. That's not like you. That's not my little girl."

14

Slowly a shape emerged on the sliding glass door of the kitchen, a man's shape that grew more and more distinct, like something blown there by the wind. Malcolm stood still, looking in, watching Kristen who was perched on a stool at the island, pouring a glass of wine. The evening news was on the countertop TV across from her, showing old photographs of Emery and Dorothy Hudson from the heyday of their careers.

A minute later, when she slowly spun around on her stool, Malcolm hid from view.

At 11:15, nipping at her third glass of wine, Kristen walked out to the end of the terrace and stood looking up at the stars. She had been thinking about walking over to the cottage to look in on Callie one last time and to say good-night, but she could see the windows were dark. They had turned in for the night.

"Goodnight, sleep tight," Kristen said quietly.

With her arms wrapped around herself, she turned back and paced slowly across the empty terrace. The grass beyond the fieldstone was heavy with dew and a gentle breeze rippled the surface of the pool. Gathering up her glass and bottle of wine and turning the lights out, Kristen went upstairs to her bedroom, but when she lay back across the bed, she was restless and in no mood for sleep. Bad weather's coming, she thought. My bones ache. And she still hadn't heard from Billy Baudin; it worried her when he was gone too long. Usually he would've been here by now. Or he would have called.

She went to the window with her wineglass, opened the shutters and looked out. She watched the starry night sky and the ocean for a long time and saw nothing foretelling a storm. Why didn't he call? Her eyes fell back to the oblong of the swimming pool, iridescent in the dark. I know what I'll do, she thought, to let off some of this tension. Getting a bathing suit, she quickly stripped out of her clothes, pulled on the navy blue tank and ran downstairs.

The water was colder than she'd expected, but still she found it wonderfully bracing. For several minutes she lay back allowing her water-borne body to drift weightlessly, feeling immersed in the black, starlit darkness. Her skin had grown accustomed to the temperature by the time Kristen climbed out into cold air. Did I hear something? The massive rhododendron rippled as if an unseen animal were caught in it. The wind, she thought, just the wind. Shivering all over, she ran to the end of the diving board and executed a perfect jackknife.

Taking her time, she swam the length of the pool twenty times, cutting the water cleanly, until finally she bobbed to the surface and came climbing out for good. In the moonlight water drops sparkled on her skin. When the breeze struck her she was covered in goosebumps from head to toe. She scampered to her towel, rubbed her hair and then down her body, lifting her legs out and wiping them dry.

The telephone rang.

She dropped her towel and ran across

the terrace into the kitchen, grabbed the phone and gasped, "Billy . . . is that you?"

A shadow moved across the lawn behind her.

"Thank God," she said, "you had me worried. I hoped it was you. Can you wait a minute—I'm dripping all over the floor?"

She ran to the half-bath under the stairs, snatched the hand towel from the rack and hurriedly continued to dry herself. "Okay," she said, returning to the phone, "here I am. I've been waiting for you to call." They spoke for a few minutes and he was telling her good-bye. "I'm sorry, too," she said. "I know these things come up, but it doesn't mean I'm thrilled. I'll see you tomorrow."

Damn it! Damn it!

She hung up the phone and, still wet in her bathing suit, returned to the edge of the pool, picked up her wet towel and ran back upstairs, kicking the bedroom door shut behind her.

She walked straight through to the bathroom, drank down half the glass of wine she poured for herself, stripped off the tank suit and stepped into the shower. She turned the water on hot, letting it pelt its warmth into her chilled muscles. *Oh, Billy Baudin, you are such a drag. Oh, Billy, Billy, Billy. You'd better watch yourself. You don't want to leave me alone too long.*

Ten minutes later she was out, wrapped in a dressing gown and robe, the bedside lamp turned on, the last of the wine poured, and a magazine opened to an article about Geoffrey Beene's fall collection. She pulled the coverlet back, threw herself across the bed and burrowed her head in the pillow. That was when the lamp went out.

Now what's happened? she thought. She sat up, groped for the switch and twisted it; it clicked. No luck. Then the power had gone off—that damned electric company, she thought. Kristen looked around at the luminous hands of her clock: it said 12:10, but it was electric too and the hands weren't moving. Feeling in the drawer of her nightstand, her fingers closed on the emergency candle she kept there and a book of matches.

Still sitting in the bed, she struck a match, lit the candle and then allowing a few drops of hot tallow to fall in an ashtray, she was able to fix the candle to it upright. The tiny flame wavered, sending its fluctuations into the trembling yellow darkness.

Her bedroom door was ajar.

She was certain she'd closed it before going to take her shower—she even remembered her hands were full so she had kicked it shut with her foot. Now the door stood open.

A tingling went through her, a tingling heightened by fear. Surely there was some simple explanation. Perhaps a gust of wind —a draft in the house had caused it to slip its latch.

Kristen was getting out of bed to close it again, when she froze, motionless. Suddenly she felt the tiny hairs on the back of her neck prickle; she held herself unnaturally still. What was *that?* She couldn't be certain but she thought she heard a door closing—somewhere else in the depths of the house.

I must be losing my mind, she thought.

Straightaway, holding the candle in front of her, she went to the open bedroom door and looked out toward the stairs. Don't be an idiot, she told herself. This wasn't the first time the power company had turned the power off in the middle of the night to work on the lines—she'd just missed seeing the announcement in the newspaper.

No light, not even the smallest sound rose in the stairwell from below. Kristen walked directly up to the railing. The saturated darkness of the night, the way shadows leapt around her when she moved threatened to unnerve her even more. But she wouldn't have it.

"Who's there?" she said clearly into the stairwell. "Malcolm? Are you downstairs?"

Kristen listened, still as a stone; no reply.

She waited. Another fugitive sound, but it was indistinguishable. It could have been anything—or nothing; it seemed to come from the kitchen. It might have been a chair or a stool being shoved a few inches across the tiles. *Was* there someone in the house?

With the candle lighting the way, Kristen went down the carpeted stairs to the kitchen, taking her time. She found the kitchen empty. Through the skylight overhead, the moonlight filtered down and the sound of her breathing seemed to fill the spacious room. Kristen glanced at the pantry, but her full attention was quickly focused on the kitchen's back door. It stood ajar an inch.

But I locked that door. I know I did. And yet, somehow, she hadn't. Malcolm must have come to the house for something; that's what it had to be. Expecting to find the cottage windows aglow with light and Callie awake, grieving but bearing up, she placed the lighted candle on the counter and hurried to the door, but the cottage windows were still dark.

Then it occurred to her that if the power was out, of course the cottage would be dark—they wouldn't have lights either. Wasn't it entirely possible that Malcolm had come over to the house, looking for candles or a flashlight?

The fieldstone of the terrace was covered with dew. And through the wet dew, like shiny smudges, she thought she could see the shape of footsteps. If Malcolm hadn't made them, maybe she had herself, running in from the pool on wet feet. Kristen couldn't arrive at any reasonable alternative. She followed the direction of the tracks up to the kitchen door.

So it was me after all.

She shut her door. And locked it. Firmly and for certain, this time. She didn't want to keep Callie or Malcolm out, if they needed anything, but she continued to feel uneasy until she had thrown the dead bolt and put the night chain on, too. They would just have to ring the doorbell.

Again, for good measure, Kristen listened. Nothing. No one else was moving in the house. She caught the edge of the ashtray containing the candle that was now little more than a stub and walked determinedly upstairs. This time her mind was on getting to bed and going to sleep. Everything else could wait until morning.

She went into her bedroom. Leaving the candle momentarily on the foot of her bed, she was slipping off her robe when she turned and ran right into him.

"Malcolm! Wha . . ."

There was a sudden angry cry and the blade flew at her in a curving slash. Before she could turn or defend herself, the honed edge struck Kristen a little below her left ear and through her throat.

She experienced instantaneous light behind her eyes. She grabbed her throat.

Blood poured through her hands and down her chest. A spout of blood. For a bare instant, she glanced down at the sudden bloodstains on her gown. Unable to make a sound, her lips stretched wide, wider and blood spewed from her mouth.

Pain seemed almost secondary until all at once it erupted in her brain. What strength she had, drained from her body. It made Kristen reel. She staggered and, for a second, almost fell. She tried to cry out and couldn't.

The razor slashed snakelike, again and again. The fancy, lace-edged pillows were spattered with blood.

Kristen gazed up, her eyes blind, expressionless. The blade flashed. Finally from the neck down, she glowed deep crimson. And round her thin neck, a gold chain had been cut into. It glittered and slid from her body.

With hardly a sound, Kristen Connell collapsed like a long red shadow, face up backward across the bed.

Day Six—Morning
The House on Hollyhock Road

15

Every now and then a star shot across the night sky and the red rim of the moon hung above the Pacific in the west.

Callie groaned, snuggled deeper into the eiderdown and reached for another pillow. Her hand slipped out across the cool expanse of sheet. Again, slowly, she moved her hand on the sheet and yet how long it took, how sluggish and slow her sleeping mind worked. It took minutes, it seemed, for the impulse to travel from her fingertips to her brain. Malcolm wasn't there.

"Mal?" she muttered. But no answer came.

She stirred. Unwillingly, her dream-struck eyes squinted open a little. Whew, she thought, I shouldn't've taken that medicine. She couldn't think clearly, couldn't concentrate. It was warm in the cottage, too warm; she was lightly perspiring. But I always leave the windows open, she thought, her dreams still hovering at the edge of wakefulness.

With an uneasy feeling, she opened her eyes. Where am I? Her mind began to clear and her eyes to focus. She realized with relief that she was at Kristen's; she had been disoriented for a moment upon waking, that's all, thinking that she was still back home in her own bed. Instead she was in this wonderful bed, drifting through space. She pulled the covers to her chin and lay back, head propped in the pillow. Hazy, still very tired . . . She could perceive shapes in the dimness and she felt instinctively that something was wrong. Where's Malcolm? she wondered again. Something had awakened her. Had it been Malcolm—going out? Still none of it quite sank in.

She thought she half-remembered Malcolm carrying her to bed. It dawned on her that she felt refreshed and wide awake, as if she'd slept for hours. All at once a lot of things swam back into focus. She remembered Malcolm's viselike grip on her throat. And the horrid story in the newspaper. "They're dead," she muttered, still incredulous. "Oh, they're dead." A feeling of raw panic went through her. Never in her life had she felt more alone, not even when her own mother died—and the realization terrified her. I've got to call, she thought, I've got . . . no, I've got to go back there. Oh, please, they had no one but me. I've got to, I've got to . . .

But I can't. Where's Kristen?

The moon drifted from behind clouds and the light flooding the room made the polished floor shine. The dark shapes began to clarify, to sort themselves out to her perception. Spindles resolved into a chair; a quivering flashing surface became a glass-topped table. Against the shadow of the window frames on the floor, a lacy dark filigree of leaves hanging from branches moved gently, back and forth, swayed by a gentle breeze.

She reached to turn on the light, but no, she thought, Malcolm might see. Carefully Callie pushed the bed covers away, placed her feet, one after the other, on the cold wood floor, and walked over to the windows. In the gloom, Callie studied the small dial of her watch. Almost five. Five in the morning. Could that be right? Outside in the distance, a dog barked across a lonesome field. Some minutes later, sounding farther and farther away, a heavy truck rumbled through the night.

That's what it had been—she knew it now—the sound of a car. That's what had awakened her. But wouldn't that be just like Kristen, to have cars coming and going all night long?

Then it crossed her mind: Had Malcolm taken the car and gone somewhere? Callie pushed herself up from the bed, drawing the comforter around her, and went to the window. No, the drive was empty. She rubbed the web of sleep from her face. Somehow her sleeping eyes had registered the sweep of headlights on the bedroom windows directly in front of her.

So—whose car had left?

I must've really been asleep, she thought. Maybe I dreamed it. She wiped her hands together nervously. I've got to tell Kristen about Malcolm. Warn her.

The stuffiness in the small room was oppressive; she kept taking long, deep breaths. It was as if all the heat of the day had gathered here. But when she tried to open one of the windows, she discovered that it was locked on the inside. Malcolm must have locked it. But why? They always slept with the windows open. Callie twisted the finger lock, threw the window up, open, and the breeze through it was cool and immediate.

She went to the next closest window and tried it—it, too, was locked tight. Callie shoved it up and the breeze gave her immediate relief. When the wind blew, the curtains billowed in and the leaves outside the window swirled as if to music. What had he been thinking?

Then, a single thought rose to the surface of her mind—maybe the car had been Kristen's. Were those the headlights Callie had seen? Had Malcolm taken her car—where was Kristen anyway?

Oh God. *She doesn't know.*

The dark sky outside her window was shot through with stars, the air calm and chill. In the west, out over the Pacific, there was lightning, eerily silent, no thunder. *She's in danger.* Turning from the window, Callie quickly got dressed, pulling on the same outfit she had been wearing before; she stepped into her sandals. I've got to find Kristen, talk to her.

She doesn't know what he's like.

I can't let anything happen, she thought. I've got to stop him. The front door, she noticed, had been locked, too. But it hardly prevented her from going out. All she had to do was turn the small thumb latch to unlock it. Still it made no sense. Why had Malcolm locked the door? With a backward glance around the room, she left the cottage.

No lights were visible in the main house. Quickly, quietly, she sprinted through the darkness and up along the side of the pool, which was lit from underneath, its surface glowing turquoise. She covered the short distance like someone running in a dream.

The front door was unlocked. Off the foyer, she entered a silent, shadowed room of dim white walls, an antique tapestry hanging above the fireplace, of chandeliers reflecting the moonlight and Louis Quinze furniture, shabby-looking, but priceless. Callie made her way to the kitchen. She hit the light switch, but no lights came on here either. The room remained deeply shadowed. Now what's happened? she thought.

She threw the switch again. Nothing. Taking a few steps to the left and feeling her way, she opened the door to the garage. By the little light filtering in she could see that the stalls were empty. But where had everyone gone?

Headed toward the staircase in the hall, she tried to shrug off her dread. Wasn't it exactly like Kristen, she told herself, to take off in the middle of the night for a secret assignation? That still didn't answer the question of where Malcolm was. Wasn't it possible that Malcolm had borrowed her car? But why would he? Where would he go?

I've got to find her.

When she reached the top of the stairs, she quietly tapped at the doors and peeked in, until she came to the door that was standing ajar. In the dimness she knocked softly, discreetly. When no answer came, she pushed the door open, away from her on what was obviously the master suite. Callie took a step into the darkness and the bare tip of her toe hit something that went rattling across the floor.

Her heart stopped. What was that?

She waited. When the moon broke through clouds, Callie saw it: she had bumped a candle stub and sent it scurrying.

That's all it was. She let out all her breath in a huff of relief.

Her gaze cut through the dimness directly to the bed and for a moment, she thought Kristen was asleep under the covers because they were rumpled up. Behind her, with a soft click, the door closed on a draft. She could feel the adrenaline pumping through her. "Kristen?" Moving with a silent tread, Callie kept drawing closer, her voice so low it hardly carried.

"Kristen?"

Another step and she saw that she was wrong. It was only a mess of pillows. No one was there. As she started to lean closer, some tiny sound disturbed the silence. It might have been a breath slowly expelled, or it might have been a spring relaxing in the gloom. Impossible to tell. Callie didn't know what it was, but her spine grew rigid and she experienced deep fear.

"Kristen," she murmured, a little louder. Her back was to the bathroom. The door was ajar. Looking over her shoulder, she gave it a slow push, peered in, and saw nothing unusual. *She's not here. She's gone somewhere.* Her fear slackening, she backed out and turned. It was then she noticed the dark brown stain on the bed.

Callie started to bend over in order to see it more clearly and noticed a book of matches on the floor. She tore one out and struck it.

Ahhhhh!

Blood!

The sight of it was so overwhelming she couldn't get her breath. She stood motionless, staring. The room was utterly still then.

It was blood—and it was everywhere.

Her stomach buckled, then grew hard as concrete. Callie struck one match after another; she could see it now. Blood splattered the wall behind the bed and hung dripping across the shutters. What strength she had, drained from her body. It was worse than she could've possibly imagined. On the bed, the great, dark, oblong shape of blood soaked the coverlet and the cry that parted her lips was less a sound than a sour hot taste that filled her throat. "Oh, God," she moaned. "Oh, my God!"

She saw something glittering at her feet and she picked it up with the tips of her fingers. It was the thin, gold necklace Kristen always wore. Cut in two.

Oh, God, help me!

As if spellbound, Callie stood gazing in terror and disbelief. *It was Kristen's blood!* There could be little doubt of that. *But where is she?* Dark crimson smears and speckles and pools of blood littered the polished floor and the small antique rug at the side of the bed. Kristen. Murdered.

Who could've done such a thing?

All of a sudden, she felt terribly sick; the night was all turning over around her.

Malcolm.

Oh, God, Malcolm, why did you do this? What did you do with her? Oh, Malcolm, Malcolm. Where's Kristen?

Suddenly the sight of all that blood whirled up around her. That explained everything . . . except, where was he?

Feeling as though she might lose consciousness again, Callie reeled back from the bed. Malcolm could be anywhere. *He could be looking for me, searching for me right now. I have to get out of here*—but she was terrified of going out that door. What if he's there waiting for me? *Get help!* she thought. *I've got to get the police!*

Her feelings of helplessness were terrifying. Unable to think straight, she started to go to the phone, but she couldn't reach it on the other side of the bed without walking through the blood.

She turned and ran.

By the time she got out of the bedroom, she felt dizzy. God, she was dizzy.

There were several telephones in the house, one nearby in the hall, but she didn't see it. At the railing, Callie had to wait until the buzzing in her ears subsided, then shakily she ran down the stairs. The trip down seemed to take too long, the air thick as water, slowing her, pulling at her shoes. All she could think of was the telephone in the kitchen.

She felt incredibly sick when she reached the bottom. Closing her eyes tight, stumbling through the dark with the single thought of getting to the police, Callie bumped against the hall table and nearly fell over it. Like a mirage in the dark, she saw the telephone sitting there and snatched it up, automatically punching in 911.

But it wouldn't ring.

She tried it again. Still nothing. She

flipped the button several times, trying desperately to get a dial tone, but nothing happened. *What's wrong? What's wrong with this damned thing? I've got to get help.* She could feel the blood draining from her head —and a horrible nauseous weakness. The line's been cut! she realized. That's why there's no phone. No lights. Unable to control it any longer, she gripped the back of a chair for support, leaned over the table and vomited.

When the first spasm passed, she turned blindly and ran through the spacious dining area, where crystal and china sparkled. She raced into the elongated kitchen, as a cuckoo clock cheerily announced the half hour. The knot in her stomach twisted tighter and tighter.

Get outside. Hurry. All she needed was fresh air, she told herself. Callie stepped out the side door and stopped in her tracks. *But what if he's out here somewhere! Waiting!*

She stood pressed in the doorway a moment, until she could get her breath and see which way to go. Then she ran. She reached the lane when another spasm bent her over and she gagged helplessly.

When she could, she hurried on as fast as she could manage. The sandy lane to the highway, glowing with moonlight, telescoped before her. Her light running footsteps seemed to reverberate with a frightening loudness. If he was anywhere close by, Malcolm was certain to hear her; it was unavoidable. Cypresses and evergreens loomed up in the dark; branches slapped against her and flew back as she ran. *Where is he? My God, my God!*

Callie came up on the end of the drive when she saw—out on the highway—headlights, still some distance away, approaching from the higher elevations. *What if it's Malcolm?* she thought. But she had to take that chance.

Hardly able to catch her breath, she abandoned the moonlit drive, darting in among the last trees, for a shortcut. *I'm here!* she tried to yell. *I'm here! Here!* When she broke into the open, she had to cross a drainage ditch; she jumped, landed on all fours and came up sprinting toward the headlight beams, frantically waving her hands for the car to stop.

The incandescence of the twin lights bloomed until she was engulfed in it.

"Please!" she screamed, waving her arms. "Stop! Help me!" Beyond the blinding light, she heard the onrush of the engine, the sudden shriek of tires on the pavement. For an instant everything seemed to hang suspended. Then she realized the car had stopped only inches from her.

"Oh, please! Please!" she cried. "Could you help me?—I need some help—My husband—" Her heart was racing. Still blinded, Callie moved through the wall of light roughly in the direction of the side of the car. *"Help me, help . . ."* As her eyes began to adjust she saw no one was in the driver's seat. The door had already opened; footsteps came toward her. "Oh, I beg you," she said, "I'm begging you."

"Callie! Callie! Don't worry. I'm here. It's me."

"Who?" she cried, still unable to see.

"It's me. Preston Harwood."

"Mr. Harwood! Oh, thank God! Thank God, it's you!"

He reached out and took her by the arm. "I'm here. Come with me."

She was conscious of his efforts to calm her down. He was repeating that if there was some kind of an emergency—he only wanted to help. Gasping for breath, she kept urgently stammering that her friend had been killed, murdered, they had to get help—couldn't he please help?

"Yes," he cut in, "you're perfectly safe now."

"Oh," she said on a long breath. "Thank God, it's you. We've got to hurry. He's still there. He'll come after me. Like before."

"Easy," Harwood said, leading her around through the headlight beams and opening the passenger door for her. "You're safe now. Get in the car. Quick. Hurry up. Everything's going to be fine now." Then he was saying, "You can tell me about it. Tell me what happened. We'll get help. Don't worry."

The door closed on her. Callie wiped her forehead with the back of her hand. Mr. Harwood went around the back of the car and a moment later, he was getting in behind the wheel. *Please hurry. You've got to,* she thought. *Malcolm's looking for me.* "Let me tell you," she said. "She's dead, oh my God, she's dead. Malcolm killed her . . ."

He shifted gears and the car moved off with a smooth, quiet lunge. Callie knew she was talking gibberish; uncontrollably, her voice began to quaver. She sobbed. "I guess you know him better than I do, but . . . I believe he's killed my friend, Kristen. There was blood all over the place. Mr. Harwood, I don't know . . . I don't know what to do. Kristen's dead; she's dead."

"Don't worry, Callie." He reached out and patted her hand. "I'll take care of everything."

"But we have to get to the police. Right away. Now, right now. Don't you see—I'm next. He's going to try to kill me."

Outside dawn was breaking, pale in the east.

"All right. All right." Harwood nodded. "You've got to settle down."

Once she realized they were already traveling quite fast, Callie allowed herself to stop pleading and lean back in the seat. In the glow of the dash lights, she saw Harwood look over at her as if still trying to come to grips with what she had said. He started, gently, to question her. "I know what you've been going through," he said. "But what happened back there?"

"I'm not sure," Callie told him. "My friend Kristen was killed and I don't know where she is . . . what he did with the body . . ."

She sat with her hands knotted in her lap and her ankles crossed, trying to stop shaking. She explained that she'd gone up to her friend's bedroom and that's where she found blood, everywhere, her friend missing. Something monstrous had happened. Harwood asked, "Did you see anything? Did you see anybody around? What happened to Malcolm?"

"No," she gasped, "I don't know."

"What about the police?" he said. "Haven't the police been notified?"

"No."

Wasn't there a phone at her friend's house? Yes, but something was wrong with it; it wouldn't work. Malcolm must have done something to the phone. He must have cut the lines. Callie answered these questions in a voice that was shocked, almost childlike. Finally, she just kept repeating, "I've got to get some help—I've got to —got to—"

"Sh-h-h, Callie," he said. His voice was so soothing. "It's going to be fine. Hush, now."

He would help her; everything would

be all right. Trying to stay calm and composed, Callie covered her face with her hands and could have cried. But she was determined not to.

"That's right," he said. "Why don't you settle back and try to relax?" He reached out and turned a knob and the dash lights dwindled to a fainter glow.

"We'll be there in a little while."

God bless you, she thought. *Everything will be all right now.*

For a few minutes, she closed her eyes. He had the car radio turned on low and its murmur was hypnotic. Callie longed to be home. They had been gone for less than a week; it seemed to her that they had been gone forever.

The highway curved away to the right through fenced pastureland. She had forgotten how lonely some of these back roads could be. There's no one around, she thought, no one passing by, not a house in sight. It was as if poison gas had passed over, killing everything in its path.

"What kind of car is this?" she asked, watching the competent movements of his hands. Why did it seem so familiar?

"It's just a car . . ." he said. He smiled

slightly as he answered her questions. "Don't worry. This won't take long. I know the way."

Now and then, she looked back, but there were no headlights behind them. She was going to be safe. *But what about Kristen?*

The road had narrowed a little, the mailboxes and fences began to be interspersed with wide fields. Once it even passed through her mind that they were going the wrong way. But she dismissed it. "We'll take the coast road," he had said. "It's shorter."

Callie cast a quick glance at his profile in the gray dawn: the clear austere features, the slight smile, the smooth, silver hair. It was getting light although the day was overcast, the sun edging higher through clouds.

The first large drops of rain struck the windows. Somewhere there on their right, beyond the trees, was the shimmer of the ocean, perpetually rolling in. We'll be there soon, she thought and she started trying to compose what she would tell the police. she was very aware of the seconds passing and she moved her feet restlessly. Something brushed against her ankle and she reached down; it was a corner of the floor mat and it was wet. She pushed it aside, but then her hands were wet.

Through the dim, rainy light, she looked down into her hands and saw blood.

What is this? she thought. Did I get this on me at Kristen's?

Blood, Kristen's blood.

Blood was all over her. All over the seat, the back of her clothes.

"Mr. Harwood, look . . . there's blood all over. I've got it all over me."

He didn't move a muscle. He didn't turn. He didn't answer.

Callie felt herself go blank, stone stammering blank.

She was covered in blood. All of a sudden, her mind made the connection: This *is* Kristen's car. *This is Kristen's blood.*

She opened her mouth to scream. Her lips moved wider, wider. It was like an instant of lightning exposing an entire landscape, etching every detail on her mind. *Blood. Blood all over me.* The figure seated next to her seemed to her paralyzed view to turn ever so slowly . . . slowly toward her. And the scream trapped in her throat began at last to vibrate against her vocal chords and the shriek poured out of Callie's mouth like a long red-silver ribbon of pain.

It was impossible to comprehend or even remember how she could have been so wrong. Horrified, her head whirled to the side, and she stared at him in amazement. "It was you!" she screamed hysterically. "Where is she? Where's Kristen?"

He looked over at her and he smiled.

It was all becoming so horribly clear to her. "Malcolm said I should never trust you."

"You know, Callie," he said, still with that hideous grin. "You really should have listened to Malcolm." He said it as if he had all the time in the world. Helplessly, she could only stare at him. "But why? Why, Kristen? How could you do it?"

"A means to an end," he said, calmly. "Everyone will think he did it. Malcolm doesn't have a prayer."

Callie sat very still, her mouth slightly open, the light of realization impossible to conceal in her eyes. "I'm his prayer," she gasped. "I won't let you . . . I'll tell . . ." And then it dawned on her what he meant to do. An insane fright sank through her.

She was beginning to make all the connections. With a sharp intake of air, she said, "You mean you . . . ?"

"Don't you know?"

He twisted toward her and slapped her —so quickly, with so little effort—that startled tears stood in her eyes. There was something in his hand, but she never saw it clearly. Again, he struck her, this time with a blow that made the darkness explode in her face. Helplessly Callie crumpled in her seat. She seemed to be falling until even that stopped, and the brilliant burst of light vanished as she lost consciousness.

16

Malcolm thought he was falling through deep water, giving his body to the cold, salty depths of blue and gold, threshing deeper and deeper into the sun-dappled shadows when his hands broke through the margin dividing life and death and he sat up in the desolate half-light of dawn, gulping air. He opened his eyes, but even the gray light hurt and he closed them.

His head was throbbing. How did I get here? He found himself on the sand with the icy water washing in at his feet. I've got to try and stay awake, he thought. In a little while, when he forced his eyes open and put his hand out to get up, he touched flesh. Cold flesh. God, what's this? he thought.

It was Kristen, and she was hardly recognizable. She was lying beside him, hacked to death. *My God, what happened?*

All at once he lurched to his knees and the pain in his head was so acute he nearly blacked out. *What the hell's happened here?*

The back of his head was bloody and his shirt was bloody and his hands. *Oh, no.* A memory awoke from the distant past—a memory of that other time when blood was put on him and a sensation of deadly unnatural cold swept over him. *Oh, no, not again. Not, again. Please God, not again.*

He turned slowly and got to his feet, feeling the ribbed sand under him. *My father did this. He must have hit me. My God, where's Callie?* He hated to leave Kristen there exposed to the elements, but he had to get Callie. That's all he could think about. A long, narrow wave curled in, drawing soft foam past him, running its white lace along the sand. *Get to Callie,* he thought. *Go. Hurry!*

He left footprints weaving toward the grassy shore, ran to the cottage and into the bedroom, but Callie wasn't asleep there the way he had left her. *What's happened? What's happened to her?* Again that sick and cold sensation came over him. Nothing in the room appeared especially disheveled.

Did she go to the house? he thought. Or did *he* take her? Malcolm tore back outside and up around the swimming pool, when he noticed that the door to the garage was standing open. Empty. "Oh, no," he moaned. *She's gone! She's gone! Is she dead somewhere?*

His head still throbbing, he ran through the house, throwing open doors, running upstairs, shouting, "Callie! Callie!" and finally into Kristen's bedroom. And there it was—the bloody bed. *"Oh, Goddamnit!"* Suddenly he knew why his father had not killed him.

He's going to blame it on me. Like before. Did he kill Callie, too?

In the bathroom, he saw himself in the mirror and realized that anyone would think he had done it. Blood soaked his shirt, blood that his father had put there. *What else has he done? What's he done to Callie?* Sudden words came sobbing and crying from his mouth, *"Not Callie, not Callie, please not Callie. Not again."* Frantic, he washed the blood off himself; then in the closet he found a man's jersey shirt and put it on.

The car was gone; Malcolm hardly

knew where to turn. Passing the unshuttered window, he saw a house in the distance, a small house not too far from the tree-shrouded drive.

It took him only minutes to get there on a run. He banged on the door, but behind him a man's voice said, "Yes sir. Good morning, Mr. Rhodes, how can I help you?"

Malcolm turned and gazed at the caretaker, who was holding some plantings in his gloved hands. "I'm Manuel, remember me, Mr. Rhodes? Miss Kristen's gardener."

"My wife. Did you see my wife?" he blurted. "Where's Callie? Did you see her?

"Is something the matter, Mr. Rhodes?"

"I've got to find my wife."

Manuel shook his head. "I haven't seen her. I saw Miss Kristen's car drive by on the road."

"When? What time?"

"I don't know. Maybe ten minutes ago."

"Ten minutes? Just ten minutes? God, I've got to use your truck. Quick! Quick! Is that all right?"

"Please don't wreck her, Mr. Rhodes. She's the only truck I've ever had."

"Manuel, call the police. Tell them there's been a murder."

"A murder?"

"Yes, Kristen's been killed. Maybe my wife." Malcolm ran to the pickup. "Listen, don't argue with me. Do what I say. Call them and tell them, the killer's in the Jaguar. Got it? Tell them about the car—the Jaguar."

The Last Dawn
The Sacagawea Skyway Bridge

17

Callie came around on a wave of nausea and terror and pain. The spinning motion in her head resolved itself into the swift movement of the car, and the rainy sweep of the windshield wipers told her where she was. I'm alive, she thought, terrified. She knew now what Mr. Harwood had done and what he was planning to do.

This time she wasn't going to wake up in her room. She wasn't going to wake up anywhere. She was going to die.

It was raining hard, and the red Jaguar was traveling much too fast, darting in and out of sparse traffic. I'm trapped in here with him. *God only knows where he's taking me.* Her hands were tacky with drying blood and there was a sticky, sick taste in her mouth. For minutes at a time, she was not really seeing the road before them, but the recurrent, haunting image of her wedding day and Kristen, lying across her bed, laughing and making fun while they awaited the ceremony.

What am I going to do?

He killed her. *And now he's going to kill me!*

Another tight curve. He swerved to avoid a car coming the other way, accelerated over a hill and down the other side. The needle sank past 90, the car vibrating. The forest was all around. She couldn't keep any sense of direction.

I've got to stop this . . . stop *him!*

It was raining, and the sky was so overcast that Callie could hardly see his face; his profile was dark, sometimes edged with a thread of gold when the lightning struck. He was wearing a starched white shirt, the cuffs folded back to his elbows. The shirt looked incredibly fresh, and it seemed so odd. How could he do what he had done and be so immaculate? Callie stayed in the corner—as far away from him as she could get.

My God, what am I going to do?

Humor him, she thought. Do whatever he says. Play for time. When she could bring herself to it, she put her hand out and touched his arm; it was hard and immovable. "The truth is," he said, suddenly, "I never meant to hurt anybody."

Callie lifted her head and they looked at each other for an instant in a flash of lightning.

"Do you believe me?" he asked.

"Of course, you didn't, Mr. Harwood."

He peered out at the sky, waiting for the thunder to follow; when it rumbled and faded, he said, "I had to do it. There wasn't any other way. Have you ever heard of the sacrificial lamb?"

A flash of lightning lit the window, making him blink. She trembled when the thunder broke.

"Have you?"

"Yes," she muttered, "I've heard of it."

"I sacrificed my son."

Tears broke and ran down her cheeks. Callie didn't move. Her spine remained rigid against the corner where the seat met the side wall. Without lifting her hands to her face or moving in any way, she tried desperately to stifle her tears. "I'm a civilized man," he said. "Malcolm always looked up to me; everyone looked up to me. I worked hard to build my business, I put in a lot of hours and at first she was . . . she was intoxicating. I couldn't help myself and then something terrible happened and it was all my fault. I love my wife very much. She's ill, you know, she's not herself. And I did it. Here was a girl who could destroy us. Can't you see the position it put me in?"

"Yes, I can, Mr. Harwood . . . I see," she replied, the corners of her mouth continuing to waver helplessly.

As if he knew she was lying, he turned his face to look at her in the gloom. Soundlessly her tears spilled over her lashes and down her cheeks. He put his hand out and touched her wrist and she automatically shrank from him. "I'm sorry that you happened to get in the way. Now you're part of the plan . . ."

Callie cried out as the thunder came again because it was right over them and the car shuddered under the shock of it; the sound crackled and crumbled away, flying into the reaches of the sky like a huge angry bird. He was telling her it was all right, it was only thunder.

And then, suddenly, something broke inside of her. She felt a loosening of the knot in her chest, and she saw herself as she was, sitting here far from home, defenseless, alone.

The lights of passing cars flashed through trees; it whitened their faces, flickered, died away. She knew he was watching her. He must have sensed something in her silence, because that was the moment he chose to say, "Don't try anything, Callie. You'll get hurt if you do." She would have to watch her own death closing in, sit still like a rabbit caught in lights and let it tighten around her. Like an embrace.

His wheels spun as the back end of the old Ford pickup skidded half off the wet pavement of the road. Easy, Malcolm thought, knowing he was driving too fast. His speedometer needle swung violently again up to 70 as his wheels spun on the muddy shoulder. Careful, he told himself. It had been a long time since he had driven a truck. If he wasn't careful he would end up in a ditch. *Callie. What is my father doing with Callie? And where are the damned cops?* Through the rain and the monotonous slap of his wipers, the highway was all black curves and luminous yellow lines before him. His hands clenched the wheel. Fifty yards down the road, he brought the pickup back onto concrete, felt the rear tires catch traction again and he floored it.

"Goddamn this rain!" Malcolm had no idea how far ahead they were by now. He only knew he couldn't run far enough, fast enough. He would be doomed if he didn't get there—no one would ever believe he hadn't committed murder—again. And Callie would be doomed, too. Callie. God, she's got to be all right, he thought.

Then he saw them, four of them, boiling up behind him—police cruisers, blue lights pulsing and blazing, sirens wailing. In seconds, they overtook the Ford pickup and whipped by one after the other and sank down the road. All right. Manuel got them. *Now, stay with them.*

Callie looked back over her shoulder at the tiny blinking blue lights in the distance. After a moment, she thought she heard the wailing of sirens. Harwood was watching them too in his rearview mirror. He had stopped talking and was preoccupied now with the blue lights.

The cruisers were coming after him. Please! she thought. Please! But Callie knew they might never arrive in time. Lightning flashed nearby, illuminating the interior of the car with its flickering electric glow. In her lucid moments she had conceived of a plan that seemed almost foolproof.

They were slowing down, curving through the cloverleaf now, moving up onto the interstate, where other cars whisked past. Light from passing cars threw rhythmic shadows on his face as they drove northward, light, shadow, light, shadow. It was not lost on her that in this traffic he would soon be forced to slow down. At the top of the ramp, Harwood gave a groan and shot into the fast lane, snaking through traffic, accelerating, cutting it extremely close.

Again Callie looked back. The police cruisers were still a mile or so behind them, closing fast. It seemed to her they would never catch him at this rate. A sign announcing the Sacagawea Memorial Skyway Bridge flashed by. Four miles ahead.

Be obedient, she thought. Do anything he says. Lull him into a false security. Already she had noticed that the early morning Labor Day traffic was slow-moving. And, as she had imagined it, he wasn't able to dart in and out of traffic quite as easily as before. The Jaguar would have to slow down on the bridge.

The porch light of a house winked by off to her right, otherwise it was difficult to see anything through the rain. They were rapidly approaching the Memorial Skyway. A stream of red taillights curved into the rainy overcast dawn; at the same time, in the strobe of the advancing headlights, she could see it—the bridge reared overhead, ancient iron fretwork painted silver against the sky. Far below, the river disappeared and then materialized on the other side. Like never before, Callie felt deeply afraid— afraid in her marrow. And there was nothing she could do. But wait. She wiped her face and eyes with her fingers, still she couldn't stop sobbing.

The lights of oncoming cars seemed to float up to her and her depth perception was unreliable. Harwood swerved toward the long upward incline of the bridge. Now clearly she heard sirens and realized that they had been gaining on them for some time. But they were still too far away. Too late.

She kept looking back. The sound of the sirens was lost in the rush of the wind and Harwood's muttered curse. The other cars hit their horns as he cut between them.

Malcolm, she thought, *where are you? Where did you go?*

If only she could get word to someone. But Callie couldn't think of any way to signal that she was in terrible straits. The campers and cars towing boat trailers were heading doggedly for vacation. Except for the fact that the Jaguar was recklessly speeding, no one gave them a second thought.

The traffic coming toward them was smeared brightly across the windshield and across her eyes. She would have to be quick. One hand throwing the door open, the other trying to fight him off. Any hesitation—she realized—and she would be crushed to death in traffic.

She was ready. She waited. Torturously, in those last few seconds, she tried to imagine everything that might happen. She had never had much luck with prayers, but she was praying now, silently and fervently. She could think of only one possible means of escape; she knew that she was going to do it, that she had to do it, and that she might not succeed.

Divert him, she told herself. Keep him talking. Her hands were cold and there was a dryness in the back of her throat when she asked, "Mr. Harwood, tell me more about Millicent Satterfield."

"That doesn't concern you."

"Yes it does. You were in love with her, weren't you?"

"Believe me. You don't want to know about her."

"Did she die naturally? Violently? How?"

He didn't answer.

"Did you hurt her, Mr. Harwood?"

No answer.

"Was she murdered?"

A long sigh. "She was killed. I've already said all I'm going to say."

"Did you do it?"

"No, it was someone else. Malcolm did. I showed you everything. Everyone said it was Malcolm."

"No, Malcolm didn't do it, Mr. Harwood. You did. Just like you killed Kristen."

He turned to her. "And that's not all . . ."

"What do you mean?"

"Too bad about your friends the Hud-sons."

She drew a sharp breath. "No."

"That fellow, Emery, was prying into things. He was too smart. He'd found out something—he was going to tell you—"

But she couldn't listen to him; she was too choked with rage. Dorothy and Emery—they had been so happy the day of her wedding. They loved her.

She remembered seeing them standing together in the living room talking to a man on her wedding day. All she had seen of him was his hands. It hadn't made sense until now, but it was as if she had been expecting the news of the Hudsons' deaths ever since.

You monster. You've got to be stopped. And I'm going to stop you!

They entered the bridge. The gray, rain-filled, morning light flickered through the ironwork at the corner of her eye.

Not yet, she thought. Wait . . . wait . . .

She was steel. They were headed into heavy traffic and he was already beginning to slow down. Callie glanced over at Harwood, at his hard features, and quickly down to the speedometer.

60, 55.

Whatever else happened in her life, nothing would ever be more important than this moment. Panic thumped in her throat.

I'll make you slow down! Until I can get out of here!

She saw the needle falling to 45, 40, 35.

Now, she thought, *Now!*

It had to be *now!*

Callie let out a scream and threw herself at him. She was all over him. She started striking him again and again, wildly, blow after blow.

"Stop it! Stop it, Goddamn you . . . damn you to hell!"

Somehow she managed to hit him full in the face and the bony edge of her hand struck the ridge of his nose. She could feel the bone crunch. His head whipped around with the force of the blow and a jet of blood spurted from his nostrils.

Harwood clapped his left hand over the lower part of his face. He yelled with shock and swung at her and missed and then his hands were full of blood. He grabbed a crumpled handkerchief from his pants pocket and covered his nose. The cloth quickly darkened as the blood soaked through it. The last thing Callie remembered was struggling with the door of the car. When at first she couldn't get it open, she twisted and struck out at him again.

Suddenly, right ahead of them in the vertical rain, she saw not the twin taillights of a car, but a jumble of taillights—and headlights too. Callie was shrieking at the top of her lungs when he lost control of the car. She saw Harwood cut the wheel hard to the left and then they were sideways in the road, hurtling toward lights, tires screeching.

With a horrendous metallic crash, they plowed into the cars in front of them. Callie felt herself thrown forward into the windshield, but the seat belt snapped her down hard in her seat. It seemed to go on and on. They had collided with other cars, at all angles across the bridge. Lost in the jarring confusion, it was impossible for her to keep track of what was happening.

And then it all stopped. At first, in a daze, Callie couldn't move. She became conscious of people shouting, running.

Pandemonium had broken out all up and down the bridge. A chorus of horns sounded all around her. People were hurt, crying out. Voices, screams were baying like wolves. She could see people running by, children being led away.

Pure adrenaline coursed through Callie's blood. Quickly, she unbuckled her safety belt and grabbed the door handle, but the passenger door was crushed and jammed tight, the window shattered. She smelled gasoline and felt the heat from the engine; she was terrified of fire. On the driver's side, the steering wheel was shoved against Harwood's chest and his head had made a large weblike basin in the windshield.

Callie's mind raced: Get away. Get away from him. Now's your chance. Get out of the car.

Using the floor mat to shield her arm, Callie knocked the splintered glass from its mangled frame. She climbed up on her hands and knees, aware for the first time of a painful drag in her left leg. I'm hurt, she realized. Oh, my God, it hurts. God help me!

She'd believed she could squeeze out of the side window to escape the car, but she couldn't. Through the gassy steam pouring from under the dashboard, Callie saw Harwood stir. She thought he stared right at her, though he could hardly have seen anything through the blood on his face. He shook his head as if to test himself.

All her revulsion came rushing back. Wild with fear, she struck at the door in vain. Then her fingers caught on the latch for the convertible top. As soon as she twisted the release handle, the top sprang open like a jack-in-the-box, and she was out, half jumping, half falling onto the wet pavement.

The rain was pouring down. Through it, Callie saw faces, white, ghostly faces muttering, "Are you all right? Hey, lady, you okay?" Amidst the steam and smoke, she saw figures moving toward her. She kept trying to say: "I'm all right. I'm all right. I'm absolutely all right."

The rain was falling harder and harder.

She struggled down the double yellow lines that divided the lanes. Having survived the accident, she had to keep reminding herself, I've got to get away, until she began to sob hysterically and the moment she became conscious of the flashing blue lights of police cars, and heard the sirens, she tried to move faster toward them. He'll come after me, she thought. The last thing she remembered was fighting him and the bridge liquid with traffic; now, at its base, it was blocked from side to side, and as deep as she could see with policemen and vehicles.

"Get back!" men were yelling. "Get back! It's going to blow!"

Behind Callie, there came the colossal *wumph* of an explosion. The force of the blast knocked her down and the bridge vibrated like a sail in heavy wind. Flame shot from the Jaguar's gas tank in a mountainous red geyser.

She lay there barely conscious, the cold cement against her cheek, the pain like a hollow beat tearing at her insides. After a long time, she got to her hands and knees. When she looked back, she saw Harwood on the other side of the fire, standing there, looking at her. His face was disfigured with blood. He had gotten out. "Stop him," she murmured. "Stop that man."

But everywhere she looked, people were tending to those who were injured.

She crawled over to the side of the

bridge and, leaning against it, got to her feet. "Help me!" she tried to say. "He's coming after me." She couldn't straighten up. The minute she tried to, the surge of pain was so intense she nearly passed out. Everything swayed; bile came rushing into her mouth and she coughed it out. She stood crouched against the railing until her head stopped swimming.

On the bridge, the flames spread across the entire width of the road, sending up a dense black billow of smoke. Malcolm pushed through the crowd to the cordon of policemen. He said to the first officer he came to, "Let me through! Let me through! I've got to get through here. My wife's up there." Wisps of smoke blew by them in the rain; the roadbed danced through heat waves before Malcolm's eyes.

"You can't," the officer said, blocking his way. "Not now. We've had a major collision on the bridge."

Malcolm turned from him, walked three paces and tore through the line of policemen. With them shouting at him to stop, he went running up the long gradual incline of the bridge.

"Callie! Callie!" he yelled, but she was too far away to hear.

She concentrated on trying to lose herself in the rhythm of putting one foot in front of the other, one step at a time. Spotlights from the cars at the bottom of the bridge came at her, shimmering off the iron beams. The rain soaked through her hair into her eyes and she wiped it away, hardly aware of her wet dress stuck to her skin. Blood was staining her front, blood running down her face. When she put her hand up and felt the cut on her forehead, it was a wide gash, feverish to the touch. Then she stared down, in disbelief, at her bloody hands.

Callie steadied herself again, her head throbbing. Over and over, she kept thinking, Get me out of this. Her arms wrapped round a girder on the long grade down the bridge, hazily trying to get things straight. The effort seemed too much; she held onto the iron beam, leaning against it. Not that much farther to go. Thirty yards, maybe. Thirty-five. The pain did not matter anymore. She was safe . . . almost safe.

Callie thought she heard someone yelling, "He's got a gun! He's got a gun!"

But the police were shouting at people, too, to stay back, and she couldn't tell where it was coming from or who was yelling, so she waited, without moving. She looked down over the railing and gasped at how close she was to the edge. The water looked so far down it made her dizzy. "Oh, God." Her voice sounded small, even to her, under the open sky, with the river rushing and crashing below. She was trembling all over.

It's all over, she thought. She saw policemen sprinting toward her up the long incline. There were shouts. Faces turned to watch her. And then, as she stood there, feeling faint—she caught sight of Malcolm running—running toward her from out of the glare of lights. His voice climbed above the others. *"Callie!"*

What he shouted was unintelligible, but his panic was obvious. Callie kept looking at him dazedly.

A shadow sped across the pavement.

All at once she heard the blaring of a bullhorn: "You are under arrest," the voice demanded. "Put down your weapon. You have ten seconds."

Harwood stepped around the iron

girder, and there he was barely two feet away, pointing the gun straight at her, smooth and black as fate. The small dark barrel of a .32 semiautomatic.

She could hardly grasp what was happening before, suddenly, Malcolm was there between them. He pushed her behind him. "Stop it, Father!" he screamed. "Stop it!"

The semiautomatic was pressed into Malcolm's chest, snug above his heart. Harwood's stare did not waver.

Callie started trying to tell what had been confessed to her in the car, but Malcolm demanded, "Quiet, Callie. Don't say anything . . . not a sound." He said this without turning his head, his eyes fastened on his father. "You'll have to kill me," he went on, his voice still loud—loud enough to carry. "You'll have to—it's the only way. I won't take the blame again. Look around you, Father. Look around. I can't lie for you anymore. Everyone will know."

The black mouth of the gun did not move, did not waver.

"It's not like it was before" Malcolm said. "You can't blame me this time, Father! No one will believe you. They'll believe me."

Rain ran down Malcolm's face. "Look around, Father! Look all around! Go ahead. Pull the trigger. If that's what you want to do."

Still the gun did not move. But for the first time, Harwood's eyes shifted for a fraction of a second. And Callie looked to see what he was seeing.

All around them were the faces of people and of policemen, who had their weapons drawn and trained on him—a muttering crowd of faces staring at Harwood.

A policeman came through the crowd. "Take it easy," he said. "Why don't you think about handing that over?"

"Don't," Harwood said, "Don't move, or I'll kill him."

Malcolm was saying, "It's over, Father, it's all over," but Harwood cut him off, grabbing him with one hand and jamming the gun up under Malcolm's chin. "Shut up," Harwood said. "Shut up." And he dragged Malcolm closer to the railing.

It left Callie completely exposed. "Malcolm," she said and started forward.

"Callie, don't," Malcolm said, barely able to move his chin.

All at once, in bare seconds, it rapidly

came apart. Malcolm threw himself to one side and pulled her out of the way. There was a moment—a frozen moment—when she saw the frantic terror in Harwood's eyes. Desperately he reached for his son, who had scrambled back. Callie caught a blurred glimpse of Harwood whirling around. He shouted out, "Malcolm, you never knew . . . !"

There was a gunshot—loud popping noise.

It nicked him. A groove of blood opened at the corner of Harwood's eye and he gave an animal shout and twisted to the side. She saw, then, that he was surrounded by police; there were guns all around her trained on him.

"No! Father! No!" Malcolm yelled. But it was too late.

Darting, nearly silent, the shadow in the white shirt ran to the iron railing. Even as Malcolm was still begging for him to stop—Harwood lofted himself over the railing and with his arms outspread, without a struggle, he was gone into the rain. Into nothing.

Time and movement froze.

Malcolm bent over the railing, watching, watching until his father's body struck the water. Over and over, he kept saying, "Please, God, please, God," even after his father was gone.

"It's over," Callie said. "I've got you."

Epilogue
Victoria, Vancouver Island

18

Once there was a boy who loved his father too much. A boy who wept when his father went away on business and rejoiced when he was home again and they were nestled in each other's arms. And that devotion did not change or waver in any way in all those young years.

And then there came a night, the middle of a cold winter night, when his bedroom door opened and there was a light in it and he was startled awake. He was thirteen. His father came through the light to him and told him that a woman was dead, that he had killed her and that if anyone found out, he would be sent away to prison for the rest of his life. And the boy said, You mean you'd never come home? and when his father said yes, he answered, Daddy, what would happen to us? I would die if you couldn't come home. And his father said, I would die, too. My heart would die.

So it was laid out for the boy, exactly what he should say and not say to the police and how the doctors would be paid to testify in such a way and the judges because his father was wealthy, and how this could never be held against him since he was underage. And the moment that it was possible he would be brought back home and he would be free. The boy said he would do it. He would do anything for his father.

They went downstairs to where it had happened, and his father mopped up blood and then dribbled and wrung it out on the stairs to make a trail to his bedroom. A trail of blood. He put the bloody knife in the boy's bed, and then they heard his mother screaming and called the police.

Faithfully the son did as he had promised through all the doctors and the lawyers and the courts. When they visited him, his mother said she loved him no matter what he had done, and his father whispered, Just a little longer, these things take time, hold on a little longer. But his father testified that his son had done it and when the boy saw what was happening, he began to claim his innocence, but it was too late. No one would believe him, not even his mother.

He was sent away; he was locked up and then when they did bring him home, he was locked away on the third floor, in a room with bars on the windows. And in the summertime, children came into the alley and yelled at him and taunted him: "Killer, Killer."

"I loved him with all my heart," Malcolm said. "And he locked me in that room. He betrayed me."

"I know," she said. "I know."

"He left me there for two more years. Callie, I wanted to tell you, but I was afraid I'd lose you."

They lay on the rag-rug by the fire and when they spoke their voices were softer than the snow crumbling from the branches outside. When they kissed each other, they were lost together for a moment. "Couldn't we start over? Marry me, Callie. Marry me, again."

"Yes," she whispered.

19

By the time he turned in toward the chapel the early September snow had stopped and the air had crystallized. Even the great spruces sparkled with a crust of snow. As if touched by the white hand of God, the land lay quiet as far as the eye could see. He maneuvered slowly down the long curve, skidding a little, and parked by the front door.

Shutting off the engine, Malcolm got out and opened the door to the backseat, where there were two bouquets of flowers he had bought in town. The red roses and white lilies were for Callie and he took them up; he would give the yellow gladiolus to his mother afterwards when they reached the house. He closed the door and went inside.

They had decided to arrive separately in order to leave together as one. Callie was waiting at the altar, radiant in a modest, blue suit. He took the three steps up to meet her and he kissed her tenderly on the cheek. Then from behind him, he pulled out the fresh flowers as promised and placed them in the crook of her arm. Back and forth between them leapt a language as silent and bodiless as electricity. He could feel himself waiting for the moment when she would look up at him with a smile of anticipation.

There were no guests, no family, no bridesmaids, no flower children or ring bearers. Only a country pastor who they thought was sincere and devout and the pastor's wife and a neighbor fellow who would serve as witnesses. Callie had asked for only one song, "Abide With Me," and it was played on the piano by the pastor's wife. Malcolm had asked if they could once again have the words from Ruth. And a traditional ceremony.

To begin, they bowed their heads in prayer. And again, as it had been before, the pastor led them through the passages, *"Entreat me not to leave thee or to return from following after thee; for whither thou goest, I shall go . . . whither thou lodgest, I shall lodge . . . Thy people shall be my people, and thy God, my God . . ."* Callie moved her hand silently until it rested in his —that was all, but the spark that passed between them seemed to quiver in the still blue dusk like the trinity of burning candles on the altar. *"And where thou diest, I will die . . ."* the pastor concluded and they repeated, *"and there will I be buried."*

Their vows were reverently spoken, the rings marvels of simplicity. When their eyes met afterwards, their looks were reserved only for each other.

Serenely happy, Callie whispered that she loved him with all her soul. For his part, Malcolm said a unspoken prayer, that they might be allowed to have their love. For now and forever, without end.

20

The barred room was silent and still. On either side of the empty single bed the lamps glowed in their pink shades and the unlocked door stood open on the lighted hallway beyond. The picture of Malcolm and his father had been torn to shreds and strewn across the room. From the stairs came a low whispering, "I hate you, I hate you, I hate you."

After a moment, a shadow filled the doorway. Evelyn Harwood stepped over Vivian's body lying all in a heap. "And now you're bringing that girl home," she muttered to herself. The scalding coffee that she had thrown into the nurse's face ran in rivulets on her uniform and into the carpet; the scissors from Vivian's sewing basket were driven into her throat.

Still muttering to herself, Evelyn soaked a handkerchief in the spill of blood and withdrew. The hem of the dotted swiss gown shifted on her ankles. Again she retreated from the room and hurried down the stairs, wringing out the handkerchief along the way, making a trail. A trail of blood. Like before, she thought. That's what Preston had done the first time after she had caught them together and she killed that girl.

She came back upstairs one last time to retrieve the scissors from the body. In the bathroom on the second floor, she tossed the bloody handkerchief into the toilet and flushed it away. Working quickly, Evelyn Harwood washed the scissors and then her hands in the sink. The force of grief at her husband's death still shook her; she had never known such loss.

"It's finished now," she muttered, still struggling to accept it. "Preston's dead. There's no one left to protect me."

In their master bedroom, where for so long now Preston had slept alone, she selected a gray velvet evening gown from her closet that perfectly caught and complimented her sea-cold eyes. She slipped it on and ran her hand over her smooth, hard hips. A comb drew her silver hair back into an exact French coil and she set it in place.

with hairpins. The pearls Preston had given her on their wedding day were clipped around her throat. Sitting at her vanity, for the next few minutes, she made up her face. When Evelyn Harwood turned toward the looking glass, it was as if she had been completely transformed. It's time for them to be here, she thought. It won't be long now.

Picking up the scissors and hurrying downstairs to the living room, she peered outside. A couple of boys ran along the sidewalk. She told herself she would know when they came because the car would sound different. How many times over the years had she stood at this window, waiting for Preston to come home, dreaming of the ways she belonged to him?

"And now you left me, you left me," she moaned. "You always said you'd take care of this . . . and now I have to."

Night had come and the streetlights were on. Wind and leaves blew in the gutter.

Evelyn Harwood turned on the porch light outside and then she went around the room pulling the window shades down, one by one. She turned off all the lights in the house. Then, grasping the scissors in her hands, she sat down in the darkness by the door.

To wait.